NELL AND AGNES

SHEFFIELD

1970

1

“Mother wanted Agnes Greystone to have her Cottage,” began Stanley. Doris, who was counting stitches, dropped her knitting and looked up. But he had stopped to light his pipe.

"Agnes Greystone? She’s not old enough. She doesn't need sheltered living, she's perfectly capable-"

"Yes, I am aware of that, Doris, but if you wouldn't mind just letting me finish- " He paused to take a few pulls: the tobacco had not caught properly.

Doris muttered something about "that blessed pipe."

"Agnes," continued her husband between unhurried puffs, " is a very worthy woman,who has led a blameless life."

"I wouldn't say exactly blameless. Not if speaking ill of one's neighbour is considered a sin. Which it is, in my book."

"Well, we've all done that sometimes, Doris my dear. Isn't it what your doing now? You know what I mean: Agnes is a maiden lady who organises the church choir and teaches in Sunday School, and has never broken the ten commandments. Not in a serious way, anyhow."

" From lack of opportunity."

"I'll pretend I didn't hear that."

Doris sniffed."Agnes does do a lot of good works, I grant you that."

"She lives in a tiny top floor bedsit, for which she can just about afford the rent, after she's fed and clothed herself."

"Yes, she's hardly two halfpence to rub together, I know. But she's not crippled, or frail, or even all that old. She rides a bike, for goodness' sake. Besides, Stan, you don't like Agnes, you know you don't. I can't think of anybody who does."

"Whether you or I like her or not has nowt to do with it. Mother liked her. She was Mother's best friend."

"Yes, they got on together. Which was just as well, because-" but Doris stopped. She must not speak ill of the dead.

"Mother told me she was leaving me the Cottage, so that I could find someone deserving, and needy, to set up in it. She didn't mention Agnes by name, it's true, but that's who she had in mind, I'm sure. She wanted that lady to be reunited with her piano. She meant me to keep the apartment for Agnes, when she comes to need it. "

Stanley's mother's Cottage had the luxury of a second bedroom, which most of the Cottages did not. Agnes, grieved by the loss of her baby grand, that had had to go into storage when she had moved into a rented room, had been overjoyed when Stanley's mother had allowed her to install it in the spare bedroom of her Cottage and come to play it there. After Hannah's death, it had gone back into storage, Agnes losing two friends at one stroke.

"Well, if that's the case Stanley, you can put someone else in it now- someone who *is* crippled, who really needs it, at this moment, who'll probably have died long before Agnes runs out of puff for the stairs. You could get Agnes and her piano one of the other Cottages, one of rented ones, anyhow. A piano doesn't need to take up a whole room, I'm sure she could squeeze it in. She's a staunch Methodist and ticks all the boxes. And you're chairman of the board. They'll always do what you tell them."

"You sound like you have someone in mind for Mother's Cottage, Doris. Someone who *isn't* a staunch Methodist and doesn't tick the boxes." Stanley knew his wife well; not as well as he thought, though, apparently, because the next moment, she astonished him by saying, with apparent irrelevance and an uncharacteristic interest in self-adornment: "I need a new outfit, Stan. And a hat. You can take me to Oxford Street."

Stanley sucked on his pipe to clear his head. Then he remembered the wedding. Their youngest son was to be married in a few months' time. Women made a fuss about such things, even sensible, level-headed women like Doris. Of course she would want a new outfit and hat, especially as this would likely be the only chance she would have of being the groom's mother. Philip was their youngest by six years, and almost thirty. None of their three older sons had ever even had a lady friend, as far as he knew.

"We've not seen Phil's new flat since he moved in," continued Doris, "but he says he's got plenty of room. And Amanda wants to take me shopping. She's a sweet lass and it might be a chance to get to know her better."

"Aye, I see that," said Stanley, aware of his wife's sadness at never having had a daughter . "You'll like to spend time with Amanda. Of course we'll go to London.

But what on earth has that to do with -? Oh no, you don't mean- Doris, you can't mean-"

"I just thought, while we're in London, we ought to at least go and see Nell. We've not been since Clive died."

"But you're not thinking, you're not saying, Doris, that I should put *Nell* into Mother's Cottage?"

"Nell is *family,* Stan. Charity begins at home.She's crippled with the arthritis, That's what our Philip said when he came for Granny's funeral. He'd been to see his Auntie Nell and he said the flat was cold, and she'd had trouble with the roof leaking and I don't know what else, and she could hardly get up the stairs to it. That's what he said. I think we should go and see for ourselves."

"Nell's not local."

"That isn't a requirement, as long as she's relatives in the area."

"She's not a Methodist."

"Her husband was."

"A bad one. And she's not-" Stanley hesitated. "Mother would have said she's not-"

"- deserving? Yes, your mother would have said that. But isn't that a description that would be better applied to her husband, to your brother Clive, rather than his long-suffering wife?"

Stanley sighed. "I'll write Nell a letter. Just saying we'll drop in when we're down with our Philip. That's all. Not now mind! I've a Bible Class to prepare. " He puffed disconsolately on the pipe, troubled by an image of his sister-in-law scattering cigarette ash around his mother's neatly kept, immaculate apartment.

"What's this week's reading?" asked Doris. "Jacob and Esau?"

Stanley just caught his pipe in time as his mouth fell open, for that was exactly the text he had chosen. The story of how Jacob had persuaded his hungry brother to sell his birthright for a dish of lentil stew had been popping in and out of his head for the last several days.

"Yes," he said blandly, recovering himself, "as a matter of fact, that's exactly what I had in mind." But it was no use pretending not to be bothered by her apparent lucky guess. He looked at his wife, and as their eyes met, he realised: *Doris knows.* How Doris knew, he had no idea; but he was certain that she did. The secret he thought he had kept for years had been no secret at all.

"But who was at fault in this story?" he asked the Bible class later."Was it Esau, who valued his birthright so lightly, or was it Jacob, who took advantage? Or was it both of them?"

2

To Stanley's relief, his son's fiancee took charge of the shopping trip.Stanley gave the ladies some cash for afternoon tea in Selfridges, so that Doris could report back that it was :"Nowt you couldn't get in Cole's for half the price", and considered himself at leisure to go and judge the quality of the orators at Speaker's Corner and walk around the Serpentine before rejoining his wife to travel back on the Underground to Wood Green, where they had left the car.

Doris spent a happy afternoon; her purchases were successful and she pronounced her future daughter-in-law to be: "Just right for our Phil."

"And the tea?" enquired Stanley. Doris sniffed "Those cakes! Half the choice you get at Cole's and half the size!" Satisfaction was complete.

Nell had invited them for "morning coffee"(which really meant tea, but in the morning, not the afternoon) on Saturday. After that, they would drive home. They had spent two evenings with Philip, approved of his flat and the wedding plans, and Stanley was determined to be back in time for his Sunday duties.

They parked by the edge of the untidy lawn that formed a rectangle in the central court of the flats where Nell lived. Stanley led the way. "I think it was this entrance," he said, stopping near a door in front of which a small child, clad only in a vest, was playing on the path. He stared at them with large eyes in a pale, thin face.

They began the three-flight climb to the top floor. As they began the third flight, they heard voices above them: Nell's and that of a young man with a foreign accent. Presently the latter came running down. He was large, dark, curly-haired and bearded, and very smartly dressed. He stopped when he saw them and squashed himself against the wall, nodding and smiling and waving them courteously past.

"Well," said Doris breathlessly as they arrived at the top, "did you see his rings and cuff links?" They had sparkled at her from his wrist and almost every finger as he gave that gracious wave.

The door opened again, and Nell smiled cheerfully at them in greeting. She looked older, Doris thought, more stooped, more gaunt around the eyes. Stanley noticed, with disapproval, the cigarette between her fingers, the lipstick, brighter and still more inaccurately applied and the hair untidier and more streakily coloured than he remembered.

The ladies exchanged kisses and Stanley shook hands with his sister- in- law. He noticed how slowly she walked as she showed them into the living room. "Teapot's warming . And I've got t'kettle on. Fifty years in London had not erased Nell's Lancashire accent. *The wrong side of the Pennines,* thought Stanley: *another reason why she might not fit in at the Cottage Homes.* He actually knew people who thought the Wars of the Roses were not over yet. He was from the wrong side himself of course.

."Shall I take your things?" suggested Nell. But they had left their coats in the car.

"I'll just take my hat off though, " said Doris, "and tidy my hair a bit." Stanley noticed for the first time that morning that his wife was wearing a hat: not *the* hat, of course, but the one she wore for church on Sundays, having given up weekday hat-wearing some time ago. Was Doris putting on airs to visit Nell?

Nell took Doris into a bedroom that smelt, Doris decided, like an oriental brothel: not that Doris had ever been in a brothel, oriental or otherwise. Nell took the hat and placed it carefully on a chair, on top of some exercise books and an English-Farsi Dictionary.

Doris laid her comb and powder compact on the dressing table next to the source of the exotic odour: an incense stick, burning slowly in a small pot. Doris had never seen such a thing before. It made her cough.

"This is Jelilee's room," explained Nell apologetically." But he won't mind. He's away till Monday."

"Jelly who?

"He's the son of an Afghan prince. Here to study English. You must have met him on the stairs. His cousin's here too, Abdullah, but he won't bother us. He doesn't get up till lunchtime on Saturdays. If you need to spend a penny, it's just next door."

Nell went to make the tea, and Doris took the opportunity to look about her. (A hat had its uses.) The floorboards were bare, except for a small middle-eastern rug. A larger one covered the bed. The thin curtains did not quite stretch across the window; a cracked pane had been mended with tape. Doris knew the flat had only two bedrooms: if Jelly-whatnot had one, and his cousin the other, where did Nell sleep? Washing her hands in the chilly bathroom, Doris noticed the chipped enamel of the bath and a bicycle lamp on the ledge by the taps. She looked up. There was a bulb in the light socket. But when she turned on the switch, nothing happened. She went back to the bedroom and tried that one. Nothing. She heard Nell, in the kitchen, coughing violently.

."I'll help you carry the tea in, Nell,"she called, flicking the kitchen light switch as she entered the room. It came on, then off, and on again.

"It's on the blink,"said Nell."They all are. And the roof's been leaking again." Doris followed her gaze and saw a large patch of damp in the corner of the kitchen ceiling. "The landlord won't fix anything. Says he can't afford it."

Doris went ahead with the tea tray into the living room, and set it down on the coffee table in front of the gas-fire, where her husband was seated in a torn plastic armchair. "There's no electric in two rooms and the kitchen roof leaks," she hissed in his ear. "And she's nowhere to sleep."

"She must sleep somewhere", objected Stanley.

Doris nodded in the direction of a bundle of bedclothes, rolled up in a corner. "On this, I suppose," she said, patting the sofa. She sat down on the end of it, which sank under her weight, pushing up the other end and dislodging a pile of magazines, that slid towards her.

Nell handed round the rock buns, and Doris bravely bit into one. "Your lodgers Nell," she said. "Do they bring much in?"

Nell laughed drily."They would, if they didn't help themselves from the kitchen whenever they feel like it."

" Must cost a bit to feed, two strapping lads."

"They do. And I had to get a pay-box for the phone. They were phoning home when I was out-" She was interrupted by another coughing fit.

"That's a nasty cough, Nell," said Doris, looking at her husband.

Nell shrugged. "I'm used to it. Now, tell me about the wedding plans!"

Wedding plans were discussed at length, Doris's outfit described, the merits of her future daughter-in-law reported on. The rock cakes were handed round again, but declined.

Then Doris said: "Are you settled here, Nell?"

"Settled ? Oh yes, I've my friends that come round. They come for tea every Sunday. There's Edna I used to work with on the magazine, Isobel who's stone-deaf and tells the same stories every week, and Joseph. Joseph writes poems." She pointed to the mantelpiece, where a poem in neat, ornate handwriting, stuck onto a piece of cardboard, stood next a framed photograph of Nell and Clive on their wedding day. Doris could just see that it was entitled:"The Blushing Bride." Nell had been a beautiful bride, there was no doubt about that. Doris had envied her for her beauty, back then.

"A romantic, is Joseph," continued Nell. "He's a bachelor. Always wants feeding. He'll polish off those rock cakes, don't you worry."

"So you'd never want to move, would you Nell, with your friends being nearby and everything," said Stanley hopefully.

"Move? Where would I move to?"

"Somewhere more comfortable," began Doris, "where the roof doesn't leak and the lights work-"

"There's a new Rent Act," interrupted her husband. "I'll see if I can't get our Philip to write some letters and put pressure on your landlord about that. He 's obliged to keep the property in decent condition. Fetch your hat, Doris, we've a long journey."

"Friends!" Doris snorted as they drove out of the court. "Nell will make friends anywhere, in the first five minutes." This was another quality for which she had envied her sister-in-law, along with her beauty and her glamorous London jobs as a journalist on women's magazines. "But she won't be able to manage those stairs much longer, Stanley, don't you see? She'll have to move, whether she wants to or not. It's cold and damp in that flat. Didn't you hear her coughing? And it's all very well having lodgers – she has to have people around her, Nell does- always has needed to surround herself- but they eat her out of house and home!" Doris paused. " If she has a decent place to live, she might look after herself better . Otherwise, she's not going to last long, Stanley. Do you want that on your conscience?"

Stanley sighed. He did have pangs of guilt about Nell, but he considered her troubles mostly self-inflicted. As to providing good accommodation so that his sister-in-law could look after herself better, well, you could take a horse to the water but you could not make it drink.

3

Agnes Greystone wheeled her bicycle along the path from the rest home, where she had just had an unsatisfactory interview with Matron, towards the Cottages. As she approached the end Cottage, which had belonged to her friend Hannah and had been empty since her death, she took a diversion across the grass and stopped by the small garden at the back.

As she had hoped, there were plenty of forget-me-nots. Agnes's favourite colour was blue. Her favourite flower was the forget-me-not, even though it spread annoyingly and took over the whole garden if you were not careful. She had a vague memory from long ago, of being among forget-me-nots in a sunlit garden where insects buzzed and the smell of wallflowers filled the air. She was wearing a white sunhat and staggered about, scarcely able to walk. Did she have a tiny watering can in her hand? An old woman bent down and looked into her face, smiling. Agnes could not have known much language at the time, yet somehow she seemed to remember the old woman saying:"Blue eyes, the colour of Heaven."

Aged four, in the orphanage, she always wanted to wear the blue-flowered dress,which was why Matron always gave it to a different child. Clothes were shared in common among the nursery children: no-one had her own. Though Agnes felt herself singled out for unfair treatment, in truth Matron was equally ruthless with all her charges. To those who liked spots, she gave stripes or checks, and vice versa. She took pleasure in cutting off any bows or frills that adorned the donated clothes before the girls wore them. She considered it her duty to stamp out nascent selfishness and vanity.

In the garden there were also daffodils (just beginning to die off) and red, orange and purple tulips. Agnes had helped Hannah plant the bulbs the previous year. The small patch of lawn was sprinkled with dead leaves, and a few bits of litter had blown in. *Really! In a place like this, you'd think people would know better than to drop their crisp bags and cigarette packets!* Angrily, she propped her bike, stepped over the low chain fence and began tidying the garden.

She was startled by a loud rapping from the window of the apartment. She had assumed it was empty. She straightened up, ready to defend herself. Technically, she was trespassing, but she considered that having looked after the garden for the previous owner, and seeing it neglected, gave her a right. A figure stood inside the French windows, beckoning to her. Stepping forward, Agnes saw that it was an elderly woman with varicoloured hair, bright red lipstick and multiple strings of coloured beads. She was grappling with the lock.

"You have to lift it up," shouted Agnes through the glass. "Lift the door up, while you turn the key."

The French door opened and the woman smiled at Agnes. "Come in!" she said. "I've got the kettle on!"

Agnes froze. Angry dismissals she could cope with; even, perversely, enjoy: friendly invitations were another matter.

"I'm Nell," continued the other. "Do come in and have some tea."

"No, no," began Agnes,"I was just-" But the woman had gone to fill the teapot. The inside of the flat was revealed to Agnes, and it stirred something inside her. Piles of magazines cluttered the floor. Books covered the sofa. Clothes lay draped over a chair.

Here was an opportunity to be useful.

4

Some people called the matron of Cherry Trees, the rest home which, along with the Cottages, was part of the Methodist Homes complex, by her first name. But to Agnes, the matron of anything was always Matron, like the matron of the orphanage; and always, in Agnes's imagination, endowed with similar qualities.

Matron at the orphanage had valued most of all, in her charges, usefulness. Agnes was not much valued by anyone for anything else. Her bossiness and sharp tongue stopped her making close friends among the other orphans. So Agnes made herself as useful as possible.

By the time she was eleven, she was pretty much Assistant Matron in all but title and pay: indispensable in helping to bath and put to bed the smaller children, to dress them in the mornings.

Then a life-changing event happened. Her teacher at the elementary school, Miss Bishop, told Agnes she wanted to put her in for a scholarship. There was a new girls' school in town that took girls up to sixteen, and prepared them for the school certificate examination, which would help to get them better-paid jobs. Most of the orphans left school at thirteen, and many of them went into service, because that gave them accommodation as well as a wage. But Agnes should not do this, Miss Bishop insisted, because she was bright enough to be a secretary, a qualified nurse or a teacher. Holt House Girls' High School was private and fee-paying, but they offered a few free places each year to poor but hard-working, intelligent girls. They took girls from eleven, Miss Bishop said, and that was the best age to begin.

Under Miss Bishop's coaching, Agnes did well in the written test of grammar and arithmetic. She received top marks for her essay entitled : "What I would like to do when I grow up," in which she described her ambition to be a famous opera singer and travel the world giving performances.

Her interview with the headmistress was less successful. In fact, Miss Collins found Agnes monosyllabic and almost rude in her answers to questions. She was a woman of aristocratic family, who expected children to be able to converse politely with adults from an early age, and was puzzled as to why her friend Miss Bishop had recommended this girl so highly. But she was also a passionate believer in women's education, and an idealist. That was why she had left her early career of teaching at Roedean to run a school for the daughters of shopkeepers and clerks. So she took trouble to help Agnes show herself in the best light. Clearly the child was fond of music. She said:"Would you like to sing for me, Agnes? A folk song perhaps? Something you've learnt at school?"

Agnes relaxed immediately. She launched confidently into: "Early one morning,"and sang like an angel. The head sent her to the music teacher, who confirmed that the child had perfect pitch, a good ear, and a voice that with training could become extraordinary. Agnes was offered a place at the school.

The school was five miles from the orphanage, a problem solved by Miss Bishop, who bought herself a new bicycle and gave her old one to Agnes. Agnes and some of the other girls had learned to ride by tucking their dresses into their knickers and messing about on the bikes that were kept for some of the older boys to get to their work. Miss Bishop kindly accompanied Agnes along the route to the school one day during the holidays, to show her the way. After that, Agnes was on her own, and on the first day of term, wobbled off precariously on her oversized conveyance.

She had to leave early in the mornings to get to school, and arrived back just in time for tea. But she was not excused any of her domestic tasks. Then an astute form mistress noticed that the child was arriving each day bleary-eyed, and confronted Agnes, who confessed to hiding in a storeroom after lights out, sitting up late to do her homework. The headmistress wrote a sharp letter to the orphanage superintendent, and Matron was obliged to distribute Agnes's chores among her contemporaries. She did this with bad grace, because they were neither as willing nor as efficient as Agnes.

Agnes fell from Matron's favour. Already resented by the other girls for having *been* Matron's favourite, and mocked for being a "swot", now that they had to do her tasks she was distanced from them even further.

On the other hand, Agnes loved Holt House School, and everything about it. She had no friends there either, but pleased her teachers with conscientiousness and impeccable behaviour.

Her aspirations changed temporarily from being useful to being clever. In truth she was not amongst the very cleverest girls, and never came top of her year in anything except needlework and domestic science (which did not count), and music. It was music that came to her rescue. The music teacher took Agnes under her wing and gave her piano lessons after school. She allowed her to practise in the lunch hours. By her third year, Agnes was playing in assembly, and accompanying the choir at school concerts, as well as singing solos. In this her two aspirations came together: being clever, at least in something, and being useful.

Outside school, Agnes sang in the church choir, and began to learn the organ. Even Matron approved of this, as being both pious and useful.

It was through the church choir that Agnes got her first job. She had passed her School Certificate with good marks in most subjects, and merits in English language and mathematics. Matron was pleased:Agnes could train as a nurse, and be useful again.

Agnes however detested the idea of looking after sick people. On the other hand, she had grown up enough to know that the opera-singing ambition could only ever be a dream for someone like herself. When a choir member recommended her to his friend Mr. Chilton, the postmaster in a village outside Sheffield, as an assistant, she was offered the job. and accepted.

Agnes was the best assistant Mr. Chilton had ever had. Her disinclination to chat, disappointing to some of his lonelier customers, was to him a virtue, because it made her more efficient. Agnes made herself indispensable once again, and when Mr. Chilton retired to keep chickens and grow fruit and veg, she stepped into his shoes. She was only twenty-two when she became postmistress, and moved out of her rented room into the flat above the post office.

5

"Matron," complained Agnes (meaning Joanna from the rest home), ," is trying to freeze me out. I've been running community singing at Cherry Trees since long before *she* was appointed. But just because it doesn't suit her convenience -in other words, she can't be bothered to trouble herself with having the furniture moved- oh, thank you," she accepted the cigarette that Nell was offering. "She makes out she's so busy all the time, but I've seen her stand around chatting when-"

"Help yourself to more sherry, Agnes." Nell was getting bored with the long litany of wrongs and injustices Agnes had had to suffer, and the character assassinations of people Nell knew barely or not at all. It was making her sleepy. "So you retired at the end of last year," she said, changing the subject."You must be enjoying the rest."

This was a mistake. Agnes looked grim. "I might be," she said angrily, her voice getting louder as she spoke. "If I'd got my full pension." It was a particular source of bitterness to her that despite her years of devoted service, this had not happened. It was all because of what Agnes referred to in her mind as the Interruption, about which she spoke to no-one. Retirement, which she had once looked forward to and planned for, had left her impoverished and without a home. "*And* if leaving early had been my own idea," she continued." But I'd another year to go.They were "rationalising" , they said.. Decided the village didn't need a post office. Now everyone has to go five miles. I ask you, is that rational?"

Luckily the doorbell rang at that moment and Nell got up slowly to answer it.

Agnes looked around the room. It had been a strange afternoon. She had refused the tea, and bustled about tidying away Nell's possessions, mostly according to her own ideas. She had consulted Nell from time to time, but Nell had taken very little interest, seemingly happy to let this stranger take charge of arranging her flat, while she herself was busy at her typewriter, chainsmoking and finishing the pot of tea. Nell's compliance was gratifying to Agnes, who, believing herself to be more sensible than the average person, and therefore quite justified in giving advice and direction to all, was used to these offerings being ungratefully received. Nell was a good listener too, and generous with the cigarettes and the sherry, which was now beginning to make Agnes's head spin. She must get home before dark. The thought of home, a poky bedsit on the third floor, with shared bathroom, brought a pang of resentment. Why was she there, and Nell here, in this cosy "cottage"with its own garden, the cottage of her friend Hannah, whom Agnes's help had enabled to live independently for the last two years of her life? How did Nell deserve this, Nell, whose cigarette ash was even now dropping unheeded onto Hannah's carpet as she came back into the room carrying some papers, and leaned over to put them on the coffee table.

Yet when Nell thanked Agnes profusely for her help, and said: "Never mind Matron. I'll come to your community singing , Agnes. There's nothing like a good sing-song,"Agnes found herself thinking she would would visit Nell again.

6

" 'Twas in the merry month of May
When all the buds were swelling
Young Jemmy Groves on his deathbed lay
For love of Barbara Allen."

Agnes thumped on the rest home piano - she had to thump to get enough sound out of it- irritated, as always, by its slightly inaccurate tuning. Some residents, gathered round, sang heartily, others croakily. Some stared into space.

Nell sang loudly and tunelessly at first, then lost enthusiasm. *Sing-alongs were meant to cheer people up, weren't they?* She flipped through her songbook.

"When the wind whistles low on the moor of a night,
All along, down along, out along lee.
Tom Pearce's old mare doth appear ghastly white...."

That song about the overloaded horse that had perished along with her multiple riders before they ever reached Widdecombe fair had always given Nell the creeps; likewise Sweet Polly Oliver dying of fever. Most of the songs that were not about death were about despairing lovers. Quite a few were about both. *No wonder the sessions are poorly attended,* thought Nell. *No wonder Matron wants to put a stop to them. George Formby would be better (though he was probably too risqué),or Stanley Holloway. They were at least cheerful and amusing. Or something more modern?* Nell knew very little about modern songs, but a sudden idea struck her. She would speak to Agnes about it after the session.

However, as Agnes slammed down the piano lid, stood up and announced brusquely that sessions would be fortnightly in future, and shorter, due to circumstances beyond her control, Nell was approached by Matron and a short, plumpish, dark-skinned man in a three-piece suit.

"Mrs. Bolton, isn't it? I'm Joanna Mann, Matron of Cherry Trees. You can call me Jo."

"I'm Nell, very pleased to meet you too. I've not long moved into the Cottages."

Yes, I've heard all about you from your brother-in-law. Nell, this gentleman is Dr. Owusu."

The man in the suit bowed slightly and beamed widely."Delighted to meet you, Mrs. Bolton."

"And I you, Dr -er-"

"Everyone calls me Dr. O. Not Dr. Ow, of course. That would make me too frightening." He laughed, shaking the gold watch on its chain that stretched across his waistcoat.

" Your-English-is-very-good," said Nell, slowly enunciating each word.

"Thank you. Most people speak it fluently where I come from."

"Which is where?" asked Nell, fascinated by this new acquaintance, and wanting to know everything about him.

"Coventry!" Dr. O laughed again. "It is true however, that I was born in Ghana. I came to Coventry as a small child. My father is a Ghanayan chieftain-"

"I've introduced Dr. O, Nell," intervened Matron firmly, "because he is one of the doctors at our local practice. They look after our residents here at Cherry Trees. We recommend the residents in the Cottages to register with them too. Alison from the office told me she brought you a form a few days ago, but you haven't returned it yet."

"Ah," said Nell."yes, she did bring one."

"The residents in the Cottages are required to register with a doctor, you know. And I think it would be just as well for you to get yourself checked over. You have a nasty cough, Nell."

"I've had it years. It's the cigarettes."

"Nevertheless..."began Matron. But Nell was enquiring of Dr. O whether he too stood to inherit the role of tribal chief, and if so, whether this would be of sufficient interest to merit a write-up in the local newspaper.

7

A fortnight later, Nell made her way slowly from the Cottages to Cherry Trees. Agnes had told her that, as it was she who had occasioned the need to print songsheets by requesting new songs, she could come early to the singing, and help with the duplicating. She hoped Agnes had not meant this literally: machines were arcane mysteries to Nell.

As she entered through the front door, she nodded to Jo, who was talking to a stately-looking woman in a wheel chair. The new resident, for so she appeared to be, sat upright in her wheelchair, hands folded in her lap, white hair pulled back in a bun, though not severely, and an expression that went with sucking lemons.

"We have a sing-along in the lounge this afternoon," Jo was telling her.

In a voice more cut-glass than the Queen's, Nell thought, the woman replied: "Thank you, but I think I shall prefer to stay in my room. I do a lot of crosswords."

"Miss Gillham likes her own company," explained a short, slight woman with brown wavy hair and an anxious expression.

Nell was intrigued, but she could also hear Agnes's curses coming from a side-room, accompanied by the ominous clacking of the duplicator. A big woman with short, grey hair and rather masculine features, Agnes was encouraging the efficiency of the machine by banging hard on the side of it. Nell hastened to offer her services.

Jo frowned in the direction of the small woman."We encourage our residents to socialise as much as possible." She wished that this woman ("Janet, my companion," was how Miss Gillham had introduced her) would go home. Too much fussing from relatives or friends, or whatever, exactly, Janet was, did not help residents to settle in. Janet had driven behind the taxi bringing Miss Gillham (her employer, presumably) and struggled, assisted by the driver, to get Miss Gillham out of the taxi and into her wheelchair. Janet was younger; sixties, perhaps, to Miss Gillham's seventies, and definitely not posh; which was probably why she was "Janet", and Miss Gillham was "Miss Gillham."

"Miss Gillham would like to explore the grounds," said Janet."I'll take her round, if that's all right."

Joanna looked doubtfully at the diminutive figure and the wheelchair. "Visiting hours haven't begun yet-" she said. But the preparations for the sing-along were underway,and she wanted to be around to supervise. "But if Miss Gillham would like that-"

Miss Gillham nodded stiffly to indicate that she would.

"-then I suppose it will be all right, just this once."

"What you need Agnes," said Nell timidly," is an overhead projector, with the words on." She had no idea how such things were operated but felt sure Agnes would manage it.

Agnes glared. "What I need is not to waste time on all this when we've only got half an hour anyhow!"

But once the session was underway, Agnes's mood improved. Audience participation was definitely better.

Jo, from her office, heard strains of Cliff Richard's "Bachelor Boy" and "Summer Holiday", and went to see how the session was going. As she came in, the music stopped, and Nell came to stand at the front.

"Did you enjoy Cliff Richard?" she asked the audience. "Yes!" they replied with enthusiasm.

"I've met him, you know, " Nell told them. "A few times. He used to come to our local church sometimes, where I lived in North West London. He came with his friend, or assistant I think he was-Bill something."

"Is he one of them?" interrupted Alf Trickett.

Nell ignored him. "I didn't know who he was, the first time I saw him," she continued. "He was wearing sunglasses. He looked like a young man I'd met in the launderette. I was in there, doing my washing, and he came in with his, and he said he hadn't realised how long it took and he'd have to get back to the record shop because his lunch hour was nearly over. So I said to Cliff: 'I know who you are! You're the young man from the record shop!' Cliff and Bill both laughed, and Bill said:'Well, he does sell a lot of records, that's true!.' And I said ' I bet he does,with his good looks!' Then I told Cliff I'd do his washing anytime if he bought me cigarettes. They were both laughing, but they didn't let on. It was only after they'd gone the deaconess said: 'You do know who that was, Nell, don't you?' I did feel a fool."

"Did you do Cliff's washing?" asked Gladys.

"No I didn't, replied Nell,"but I'll tell you what- the next time he came to church, he brought me two packets of Rothman's. A very nice young man."

"Is he," repeated Alf, “one of *them*?"

Nell looked blank. "One of whom?"

"He's not married, is he? They say he might be-you know-one of *them*."

"Shut up, Alf!"said Gladys.

"Page six," announced Agnes. "Widdecombe Fair."

At teatime there were several favourable comments: "We like Cliff", "Nell made us laugh."

"I'd have liked a bit of George Formby though," said Alf. " 'When I'm cleaning winders'. "I were a window cleaner, you know. I saw some things, I can tell you."

"You never were,"contradicted Bert. "You told me you were a baker."

"I were too,"said Alf. "Before the baking. I had a portfolio career, me. My uncle- he were a window cleaner-he had an accident. I were just leaving school and I had to go and help- go up ladders for him."

"Budge up there, Alf," said Eric. "Make way for the new lady." Miss Gillham was manoeuvring her wheel-chair up to the table. Sing-alongs were one thing. Tea and cake were something else.

Alf cleared a space. "Well," he continued, "I were workin' on this flat on't first floor, and t'curtains weren't drawn like, and there were this woman, stark naked, dancing round t'bedroom. Well, in come her 'usband and says-"

"Alf ! There's a lady present," remonstrated Bert.

Everyone turned to look at the new arrival, who sat erect and composed in her chair. They noticed her grey suit over a silk blouse (who wore a *suit* indoors, when they weren't going anywhere?), her pearls (real?) and the lemon-tasting expression. Was the expression because of Alf, or was it a fixture?

" 'Ow do?"said Alf.

"Good afternoon." Miss Gillham looked around her, nodding graciously to each in turn.

She's not so bad, thought Gladys. *Even if she does have a plum in her mouth. As well as a lemon.*

"Oh dear me, I beg your pardon," said Alf in strangled tones. " *That* were what I meant to say. Good *arf*ternoon. How do you do?"

Gladys kicked him sharply in the shin, which hurt her arthritic toe badly. "Pleased to meet you love,"she said to the newcomer. "Have a piece of cake."

8

"Will your anchor hold in the storms of life,
When the clouds unfold their wings of strife?
When the strong tides lift, and the cables strain,
Will your anchor drift or firm remain?"

Agnes bashed the piano. Stanley surveyed the congregation, assembled in the Cherry Trees drawing room. As Superintendent of the Methodist Church in Sheffield, he did not conduct worship every Sunday at The Methodist Homes, but as Chairman of the Board, he sometimes put in an appearance. He looked at his sister-in-law, who was singing with discordant gusto:

"We have an anchor that keeps the soul
Steadfast and sure while the billows roll,
Fastened to the Rock which cannot move,
Grounded firm and deep in the Saviour's love -"

It will surely hold in the floods of death,
When the waters cold chill our latest breath-"

You could not fault Nell on enthusiasm. He had to say that for her. But Matron had hinted that there was something she needed to talk to him about after the service, some tale about Nell and the doctor and the cleaner.

As coffee was being served, he was astonished to see Nell deep in conversation with Agnes Greystone. He was on his way over to talk to them when Matron caught up with him.

"They seem to get on like a house on fire," said Jo.

"So I see, Matron. It is a bit of a surprise."

"Which brings me to what I need to talk to you about."

"Those two getting on well?"

"No. Fire. "

This put Stanley in mind of his pipe, and its soothing balm. It would be antisocial to light up in the drawing room.

"Our head cleaner, Mrs. Charnock, complained to Alison in the office."

Doris had told Stanley that it was essential for Nell to have Mrs. Charnock, or one of the other cleaners, for at least two hours a week, though Nell herself had demurred. The cleaners' main duties were at Cherry Trees, but the residents in the Cottages also had the option of employing them. In addition to her pension, Nell received a rent allowance from the council, paid to Stanley, as landlord and owner of the property. Stanley used it to pay Nell's utility bills, and it also covered the cleaner.

"Mrs. Charnock has complained that the carpet is covered in cigarette ash. It's hard for her to get it out, and it's becoming ingrained. And she's concerned about the cigarette ends. She found one in the bin, apparently, still smouldering. Also tea leaves in the bin, unwrapped and still wet, getting all over everything in the dustbin. And she doesn't think that Nell has used the shower at all. It's still got the plastic wrapped round the new unit that was fitted after old Mrs. Bolton died."

Stanley frowned. It was likely Nell did not understand showers. Indeed, he and Doris had only ever had baths. He was not sure he would know how to operate a shower himself. "What's she been using then?" he asked.

Jo cleared her throat, and lowered her voice."We don't think," she said,"that Nell washes very much."

Stanley's teeth clamped around an imaginary pipe, and chewed on it. "Well *I* think, Matron,that these are not things for you to concern yourself about, Surely they are matters for Mrs. Charnock and the office to deal with."

" But you see, Reverend Bolton,- these things don't come strictly under my remit, I agree- but there's something else which, I believe, does. It concerns the health of our residents ."

Stanley looked up and raised a reluctantly enquiring eyebrow, taking some imaginary pulls on the imaginary pipe.

"Nell has such a dreadful cough. And she's not been seen by a doctor. She's not signed on with one yet. She comes over to Cherry Trees a lot now, to chat to our residents- and I wouldn't want to stop her for a minute- they like her, you see, she cheers them up. I like her myself. Really, she is most welcome here. But if the cough hasn't been investigated...There's this new 'flu around, we're beginning to hear about....One can never be too careful....So I thought you, Reverend, being family, might have a word."

Doris, thought Stanley. *It was your idea to bring Nell here. This is a job for you.*

9

"You were a beautiful bride, Nell." Doris was standing in front of the photograph that had inspired Joseph's poem. The picture and the poem-in large, flowery handwriting-now both adorned the mantelpiece in Nell's new apartment.

"We both were," said Nell kindly but untruthfully."Those were the days, weren't they?"

"For you perhaps," said Doris. "You and Clive were in London. I was in Fleetwood, remember, struggling with our Angus, who never slept through till he was three. All under the watchful eye of our mother-in-law."

"She could be a bit of a tartar,"said Nell, though privately thinking that, when it came to the disapproval-from- mother-in-law stakes, she herself had drawn the short straw.

"Remember the polish?" said Doris.

"Oh, yes. I admired the shine on your dining-room table."

"You said:'What a lovely shine, Doris' and asked me what polish I used.
'Polish!' says Granny, 'polish! Waste of good money!'"

"All you need-" they finished together, laughing, "is elbow grease!"

"Oh dear," said Nell. "And your furniture was so beautiful. She should have seen *my* tables and chairs."

There was a slightly awkward silence, then Doris said: "Nell, Stanley asked me to talk to you about one or two things. The shower, for example. We're not sure if you know how to use it. I'm not very good with them myself, though I did manage to get the hang of the one in our Philip's flat. Alison from the office could show you how it works, or, Matron said, one of the Cherry Trees careworkers could come and help you shower-"

"No!" said Nell, horrified. "I'll manage, don't you worry. I've not got round to it yet, that's all." With sudden inspiration, she added, "Agnes can help me with it. Agnes has been very helpful, with shopping and so on."

Nell tried to avoid the butcher's and greengrocer's vans, which came round regularly, but were expensive. The baker's van was pricey too, but tempting. She looked forward to the weekly minibus trip to the shopping centre, but could only secrete one sherry bottle under the groceries in the basket-on-wheels that Doris had given her, without making it suspiciously heavy when the driver lifted it onto the bus. Agnes was happy to fill the gap.

"Perhaps Agnes could help you with signing on at the doctor’s too," suggested Doris. "You really must get that done, Nell."

Nell assured her that she would, and Doris went away, wondering at the rapport Nell and Agnes appeared to have struck up. It was only when she got home that she realised she had forgotten to mention the tea leaves, and the cigarette end business.

10

Nell did not trouble Agnes with the doctor's registration, but filled in the form and walked , slowly and painfully, the quarter of a mile to the surgery to give it in. She was told she would have to come back for a check-up, which turned out to be, not with her friend Dr. O, but with a woman whom Nell privately labelled the Battleaxe, because she was large, impatient and terse. The Battleaxe pronounced that Nell had nothing infectious, ordered her to cut down on cigarettes, and scribbled a prescription.

Nell crumpled the prescription and stuffed it in the bottom of her handbag.

Medicines generally upset her stomach. Extra strong peppermints, Tunes and Fishermens Friends were her staples. As to the smoking advice, she reflected on her walk home that she need not take it, since the Battleaxe herself appeared not to have done so. Nell had noticed the nicotine on the doctor's fingers.

At home, Nell took some scissors and went into the bathroom. She cut the plastic wrapping off the new unit, and after some false starts, managed to get it to spray enough water around to look as if it had been used. That should satisfy Mrs. Charnock, or Alison, or Matron, or Doris, or anyone else who happened to look in.

Exhausted, and with an annoyingly wet head and shoulders, Nell turned her favourite armchair, with footstool, toward the French windows, where the warm afternoon sun was streaming in. She poured herself a glass of sherry, settled in the chair with her feet up, and lit a cigarette, that burned away in the ashtray as she drifted off to sleep.

When she woke, the sun had gone and she felt cold. The dusk brought with it gloomy thoughts.

When the weather was warm and summery, Nell's cottage was a cheerful place to be. The garden faced south and caught the sun. There was a bench out there for her to sit on, but she only usually did this when other people were about. If her neighbour Ruth, from next door but one, had grandchildren visiting, she invited them all into her garden for tea, orange squash and chocolate biscuits. She had a collection of old Bunty annuals and some exotic nick-nacks (gifts from the Afghans), and while the older child and her granny amused themselves with these, Nell took the younger one across the lawn to a small copse, to look for the elves and fairies who lived there, telling her tales about them the while.

Ruth was happy to share her grandchildren. She knew that Nell rarely got to see her own. One of Nell's sons lived in London, the other in Australia, and in any case, neither had any children. Her daughter, apparently, was married to a Welsh farmer and lived in Angelsey. She had three young children and a difficult husband who refused to speak English and had made Nell feel distinctly unwelcome when on the rare occasions she had braved the difficult journey to get there.

Next to Ruth, on the end of the row of four cottages, lived George. George was cheerful and friendly, but unable to remember, when Nell spoke to him, that he had ever spoken to her before, and so he always asked her if she had just moved in. He then told her that he had only just moved in himself, though Ruth assured Nell that he had lived there some years. Nell had twice invited George to tea also, but he had forgotten to come.

Nell had so far failed to discover the name of her immediate neighbour. Ruth thought her surname was short and began with a C, but did not know anything else about her.

Miss- or Mrs.- C rarely appeared out of doors and, if Nell tried to speak to her, retreated back inside. She could sometimes be seen at her French windows, glowering at the children if they were about.

Doris visited fortnightly, and Agnes once a week. There were the community singing, the Sunday services, and the weekly trip to the shops. But Nell had been used to a constant buzz of people around her for nearly all of her life. She felt lonely.

Nell never allowed herself to dwell on melancholy thoughts for long. She made three plans that evening. The first was to invite one of her London friends to visit.Some of them had said they would. Edna, Nell thought, would not be brave enough to make the journey, though she had written several letters telling Nell how much she missed her. Isobel would be unable to find her way to the station. The lodgers had promised to visit in their holidays from college, but she could hardly have two young men to stay here, even if they had not been busy convincing their fathers that they were studying English, and chatting up au pairs. But Joseph -Joseph had earned free rail travel form his long service as a booking clerk, and often toured the country, sleeping on different trains. Would it cause a scandal if she had Joseph to stay? Surely not, at their age?

Feeling more cheerful, Nell made tea, cooked herself some supper, and went to bed.

11

The next afternoon,when Janet said goodbye to Miss Gillham after her usual visit (always from 2pm till 3pm) and headed back to her car, a voice called out to her: "You're very faithful!"

Janet looked around her, wondering if the remark were meant for someone else. But only one other person was present in the carpark: the woman with the smudged lipstick and multicoloured hair. Janet had seen her about, but never spoken to her. She smiled, questioningly.

"Visiting your friend, Miss- Gillham is it? Regular as clockwork."

"Oh well," said Janet, "she's my best friend, you see." She noticed a letter in Nell's hand. "Can I post that for you?"

"That's kind, said Nell, "but I need stamps. If you could just drop me at the Post Office, I'll get the bus back." Here was an opportunity, she thought, not just to post her letter, but to indulge her curiosity about Miss Gillham.

She did not waste it. "Have you known each other a long time? " she asked as they drove along, "you and Miss Gillham?" Clearly, they could not have been at school together.

Janet seemed to read Nell's thoughts. She looked sideways at her passenger."It sounds odd, doesn't it, saying that we're friends? What with us coming from such different stations in life. My father was a factory worker, hers a high-ranking naval officer, and honorary surgeon to the king. Her mother's cousin was married to an earl."

By the time they reached the Post Office, Nell had learned that Miss Gillham had been the youngest of three sisters, a highly intelligent girl who, most unusually in those days, had taken degrees in both mathematics and classics at Bedford College London and Cambridge, and received a first in both. Women had not been allowed to take degrees much before then. On the way back (for Janet decided to spare her the bus journey), she learned that Janet had come to the family as a maid, when Priscilla-Miss Gillham- was already quite grown up, and only at home during vacations.

"What did she do with her degrees?" asked Nell.

"Civil Service," said Janet. "And -war work, later." She glanced sideways at Nell, again. "I stayed with her parents-her sisters had long before married of course. Miss Gillham's father died soon after she left home but her mother outlived him by many years. When Miss Gillham retired, I moved with them both up here. It was what she'd always wanted, a cottage in the Peaks. She was a rock climber. until the accident. "

"A rock-climbing accident?"

" She got over it well enough at the time, but then, with age - that's why she's in a wheelchair. "

"What an interesting life," said Nell, though in truth she did not think either the Civil Service or rock-climbing very interesting pursuits. But there might be room for embellishment in this life story. The unspecified "war work" could possibly be developed, to add some drama.

It was Nell's second new plan to make a collection of the life stories of all the residents in the Cherry Trees and the Cottages; of all those who were willing to impart them, anyway. She could not imagine Miss C doing any such thing. Nell had begun several attempts to write her own life story, but found it led to sad reflections on the sadder parts of it. This would never do. Concentrating on other people's biographies would avoid that danger.

12

"My nephew is a solicitor," Nell informed Agnes. "The one who's getting married soon."

"Reverend Bolton's son, you mean? Are you going to the wedding?"

"I've been invited, but I don't know if I will. It's a long journey, and it'll be a long day." There was also the vexed question of paying for a new outfit and an overnight stay.

"I wouldn't bother. Overrated, weddings," opined Agnes gloomily. "People should have better things to do with their money. Half the time the marriage doesn't last five minutes. People these days-"

"I was going to say," interrupted Nell, anxious to avoid yet another litany of what was wrong with people these days, "is that if I have a word with Stanley, he could get Philip-my nephew- to write a letter for you. About your pension. It can't be right that you don't have a full pension, when you've worked all those years."

"There was a gap," explained Agnes reluctantly. "I was -ill for a while."

"Well, nobody can help being ill, can they? It must be worth a try-"

"It would mean dragging everything up. They might want to know-too many things." Agnes changed the subject. "I had some money once, you know. I bought a little house. A cottage by the seaside. You can put that in your story."

They were sitting in Nell's garden, having tea and crumpets, and Nell was making notes for Agnes's lifestory, to add to her collection. They had covered the orphanage, Holt House School, and the Postmistress job, but progress had come to a standstill. Nell seized on this new nugget hopefully. "Where was it?" she asked, scribbling on her pad.

"Robin Hood's Bay. It was tiny. Two up, two down, bathroom and kitchen. A little garden outside. Beautiful views. I didn't live in it of course. I lived above the Post Office, but I took my holidays there. It was my investment. I was going to retire there. And would have done, but for the rat."

"The what?"

"That was my illness, you see. Rat-poisoning. I don't mean I swallowed rat-poison. I was poisoned *by* a rat."

"Did it bite you?"

"Savagely,"said Agnes, sounding quite savage herself.

Nell, never comfortable with disaster stories, changed the subject. "How did you come into the money, if it's not a rude question?"

"My grandmother-I think she must have been the old woman I remember in the garden-had two children, Doreen and Roland. Doreen was my mother. She died when I was three. Topped herself, probably," she added dispassionately. "But I don't know. No-one's ever told me. My father wasn't on the scene. Nobody knew who he was. Except my mother, presumably. I must have stayed with my grandmother, I suppose, but then she died not long after. That's when I went to the orphanage. Well, Roland was still living with his mother when she died-so

I found out later-and I do have vague memories of him: giving me piggy backs and rides round the garden in a wheelbarrow. Roland went to Canada and did very well for himself. To cut a long story short, he made a lot of money and died. Relatively young. Heart problem. I didn't know any of this, of course, until one day, out of the blue, I had a letter from my cousin Evelyn, Roland's daughter, who I didn't even know existed. I've still got the letter. I'll bring it and show you."

"How exciting! A long lost cousin!"

"She still writes sometimes. Says I should go and see her. As if *I* had the money to do any such thing! She should come here if she's bothered! Anyhow, it turned out Uncle Roland had left me some money."

"That was good of him. "

"I suppose," acknowledged Agnes, grudgingly."It wasn't a fortune. Enough to put a deposit on the cottage. I paid the mortgage out of my salary. Scrimped and saved. I'd not much else to spend it on, except necessities. I've never been a spender, unlike some people-"

"You must have had good holidays there," said Nell quickly, to forestall another tirade.

"Oh yes, I did. I did, for a few years. I'd nearly paid the mortgage off, too, when…"

"The rat bite?"prompted Nell, nervously.

"I was ill for months. Couldn't work for two years. The job at Mexborough had gone by then, of course. But I found another post in the end."

"The one you retired from last year?"

"Yes."

"I wonder, Agnes," said Nell, "if you've got any little anecdotes we could put in? Stories about customers, you know. People like that sort of thing."

"Oh, I've plenty," said Agnes. "The stupidity of some people knows no bounds. There's nowt as queer as folk."

"Save me and thee,"agreed Nell, both adding silently:"And I'm not too sure about thee."

But Agnes was too tired for anecdotes that day. it was time to pour the sherry.

13

Nell accosted Dr. O as he hurried back to his car from Cherry Trees. He greeted her with a wide smile, concealing a slight nervousness. This was brought on by the fact that the last time he had spoken to Nell, she had told him she was counting on him to take part in the musical sketch she and Miss Greystone were planning as part of a “concert”. "Mrs. Bolton! How lovely to see you! What can I do for you today?"

"Oh, nothing thank you, Doctor. I'm fighting fit."

"Apart from the cough and the arthritis. You know, Mrs. Bolton, none of us likes to confront our own mortality, and we may be afraid of what investigations may discover. But sometimes these investigations mean we can catch diseases early, and take action that prolongs our life. It is a mistake to ignore symptoms."

Nell made a dismissive gesture. "I just wanted to ask you a question, Doctor, about a friend. If someone is bitten by a rat, could it make them ill for a long time, say a year or more?"

"There's such a thing as rat-bite fever," said Dr.O, "but one would expect the patient to recover from that within a week or so. And a tetanus injection would be advisable. Has your friend had one?"

"I expect she did. It happened some years ago."

"Well, in that case the rat-bite should not have caused a major problem, unless the rat were carrying some ghastly disease- bubonic plague, for example. But that would be unlikely in this country."

"Thank you, Doctor. About the musical-"

"Really, I have very little experience in that kind of thing-"

"Not even a school play?"

"Not since I was four, and that-was not a great success."

"Oh dear. What sort of play was it?

"I was First King in the Nativity. I had to say:"We come bearing gifts. Mine is gold, which represents royalty."

"That's quite a mouthful for a four-year-old. A lot of children are shy at that age."

"I was not shy. I remembered my lines and I said them in a 'big, loud voice', just as the teacher had told me. But you see, my mother- she was so proud I had been chosen for the part, she found me a magnificent crown. She borrowed it from a friend, I think. But it was too big and it slipped down over my eyes just when I went to kneel down by the manger with my gift. I fell over the manger, tipped it sideways, and the little Lord Jesus fell out."

Nell laughed sympathetically. "You didn't get told off I hope. It wasn't your fault."

"The teacher was kind. And the audience gave me a special clap. But my older brothers wouldn't let me forget it for months."

"I'm sure nothing like that will happen in our musical. And you would only have to play yourself-"

"You must excuse me, Mrs. Bolton. I am late for my patients."

As he hurried away, Nell decided she would have to work on Dr. O. The doctor playing himself was essential to their production. If he could sing, that would be useful too, as they were short of male voices. And if he starred in the performance, as Nell suspected he might, the Nativity disaster would make a nice anecdote to add to the review she intended to get into the local newspaper.

Nell also decided to tackle Agnes on the subject of the rat-bite. The story was odd. Had Agnes made it up, or exaggerated the consequences? If so, why?

14

"Well, I never did! The cheek of the woman!"Stanley was seated at the breakfast table, reading a letter. "Would you believe this, Doris-" he continued, but then he abruptly stopped. She had taken plates out to the kitchen, and possibly had not heard him. The letter alluded to things about which he had never spoken to Doris, that he had thought she knew nothing of. Perhaps he should still keep them to himself. On the other hand, during their first discussion about Nell and his mother's flat, he had realised that Doris *did* know all about the unfortunate business, so what was the point of keeping it to himself any longer?

Doris decided the matter by coming back from the kitchen and demanding:"Would I believe what?" The woman had super-human hearing.

"Do you remember Hubert Scully?"

"Hubert Scully in the church choir? He had a lovely baritone voice. Bit of a charmer. Surprised us all by being sweet on Agnes for a while."

"Was he?" Stanley sounded astonished.

Really! thought Doris. *How could her husband be so obtuse about things that were plainly obvious to the average person. Well, the average woman, anyway.* "He pretended to be, at any rate. I never did trust that man. And I was right, wasn't I? He ended up in prison for fraud."

"That was some years later, but yes, he did."

"And before that, he said he owned a building firm and would build the Cottages, then left them hardly started and disappeared with the cash."

Well of course Doris knows that part of the story, thought Stanley. *It was in the local newspaper.*

"All those poor people who invested their money in the building fund, thinking they'd get a pay-out when the Cottages were sold!" continued Doris. "They lost every penny." She paused. "You lost a good bit yourself, Stan. That money from your uncle."

"It was a bad business," agreed Stanley, "a big mistake on my part. I trusted Hubert. He seemed so…respectable. I do regret-it didn't matter about my own money-but I do regret encouraging other people to part with theirs."

"Including your brother. Including Clive."

So she did know. Stanley said slowly:"I did what I thought was right at the time."

"Or what your mother thought was right."

" What makes you think Mother -"

"I wasn't eavesdropping, Stan, really I wasn't. I was in the hallway, in the dark, being very quiet, because I was wheeling our Philip up and down in his pram, trying to get him off to sleep. The door was open a crack and you weren't talking quietly. I was worried you'd wake him up again."

Doris had heard her mother-in-law discussing with Stanley a legacy left by an uncle, the prosperous owner of a furniture business. He had left some money to Stanley and some to Clive, leaving out their elder brother Ernest who was established in the wine trade and therefore persona non grata to their tea-total uncle, and their younger brother Bill,who was in disgrace for other reasons. "Now Stanley," his mother had said, "I don't want Clive to have his share of that money. I mean, I don't want him to have it to waste. He'd drink and gamble it away, like as not." Stanley must have opened his mouth to protest, because she continued: "Oh yes! Don't think I don't know about our Clive's habits."

"You can't keep the money from him, Mother."

"I'm aware of that. I don't say we should keep it from him. But you could maybe invest it for Clive. Find a reliable, worthy sort of business for him to put it into. One that would make a profit for him, in the longer term."

"Oh, I could find that," said Stanley. "As a matter of fact, I've a worthy cause in mind at the moment. But I doubt Clive will listen to me."

"He won't if he's given the choice. You could just tell him that Uncle John left the money on condition it's put into some good Christian business -like the one you have in mind. I'm sure your uncle *would* have said that, if he'd thought of it. I'm sure he would if he'd known what else Clive might use the money for."

"There'll be papers, Mother.."

"Papers! Clive doesn't need to see papers. You're sole executor, Stanley.Clive'll take your word for it."

"Of course, " Doris said now," your mother may have been right about Clive wasting the money. I don't say he wouldn't have done that. But he *might* have spent some of it on the family, or paid off some of his debts before they got bigger and caused all the trouble that came later.

He should have had the choice, I say. Still," she added,"Nell has the Cottage now, which is only just, don't you think?"

"Yes. You're quite right, Doris, about all of it. I was wrong to do what I did. Though I didn't think so at the time." Stanley sat, head in hands, staring at the table. He looked mortified.

" If it's any consolation, " said Doris, "*I* didn't think so at the time, either. I'd have said something if I had done." She patted his shoulder and said briskly: "Water under the bridge, Stan. What we need is another pot of tea."

While it was brewing, she read the letter that Stanley had received. It was from Hubert Scully's daughter. (Doris did not remember anyone ever mentioning that Mr. Scully had a daughter). Stan was right: the woman *did* have a cheek. She said that she and her father were back in the area, and he was now very frail. She requested,(of all things) that he should be allowed to have one of the Cottages!

15

Every Friday afternoon Janet and Miss Gillham took a trip out by taxi (since the wheelchair would not fit into Janet's car.) Their favourite destination was the Lavender Tea Room in Bakewell. On this particular Friday, around the middle of August, Miss Gillham had invited Nell and Agnes to join them. The purpose was to discuss the musical performance Nell and Agnes were planning for the autumn, with which they hoped to raise money for Christmas treats.

The ladies had reserved seats near the back window, where they had a view of the garden, and where Miss Gillham's wheelchair fitted neatly into an alcove and would not be in anyone's way.

Every table had a clean, white, lacy cloth and a small vase of flowers. The crockery was pretty, and matching. The only fly in the ointment, Agnes decided, was a small boy at the next table with untidy hair and a face smeared with chocolate cake, who seemed unable to stay in his seat. "Orlando," his mother warned. *(Orlando?* thought Agnes. *How could you expect a child to behave with a name like that?)*.. "What did I tell you, Orlando?"

"No ice-cream if you don't sit up!" chimed in the boy's father.

Orlando ignored them both, draped himself sideways over the seat of his chair, and stared at Agnes as she wolfed down four dainty, crustless sandwiches in quick succession. In anticipation of the afternoon treat, Agnes had had no lunch.

“Bread's a bit dry,"she observed, and, fingering a cold sausage roll, added: "and you'd think they might have stuck these in the oven."

"Well, I'm thoroughly enjoying my tea,"said Nell. Not liking anyone's feelings to be hurt, she looked anxiously at Miss Gillham.

That lady's face, however, showed no expression other than its usual lemon-sucking one. The lemon-sucking expression, Nell had discovered from seeing photographs of Miss Gillham in her teens and twenties, appeared to be due to the natural structure of her face. The poor girl must have felt it sorely at the time.

"Perhaps the veal and ham pie will be more to your taste," suggested Janet to Agnes, with an archness that was lost on the latter.

"Never liked that," snapped Agnes. Janet caught Nell's eye, and rolled her own.

"Now, the musical," said Nell,"we must get down to discussing that-" But she was interrupted by heavy gasping sounds. Agnes was clutching her chest and struggling for air.

"Oh my goodness! Is it the sausage roll? Have some tea-" Nell hurried to Agnes's side, and refilled her cup, while Janet slapped Agnes quite hard on the back. Miss Gillham summoned the waitress and ordered: "A paper bag, quickly! Now, Agnes," she continued when the girl hurried back with it, "put that over your face and breathe in and out slowly. Nell, put the tea cup down and help her. Slow, deep breaths Agnes, and you will soon feel better. Follow my count..."

Gradually, Agnes's breathing returned to normal.

"I think she will be fine now," pronounced Miss Gillham.

"Yes, yes I will. No need for a fuss." Agnes glared reproachfully at her companions, a few concerned spectators from other tables, and the scared young waitress.

"Perhaps, young lady," Miss Gillham addressed the girl,"you would fetch a fresh pot of strong, hot, tea. Our friend may need some, with plenty of sugar. She's had a shock."

"No need, no need for a fuss...It was just...it was...I don't know what came over me....I just saw ...I just saw.. ..." Agnes's suddenly grasped Nell's arm and whispered: "It was the Rat! I saw the Rat!"

"*Rat*!" The outrageously-named Orlando, who had crept up quietly and unnoticed behind the two ladies, to investigate what was going on, shouted "Mum! There's a rat! There's a rat, Dad! It might be under the table!" he dived beneath the table, then emerged the other side, and scuttled across the floor to the next one, almost tripping up the waitress on her way back with the teapot.

Other people were searching now, under their tables and chairs, on the window sills, behind the curtains. Someone even lifted the lid of a sugar bowl.

"What on earth are you doing?" The manageress had arrived on the scene and flapped her tea towel at Orlando. "You come out from under there, right now!"

Orlando came out. "There's a rat," he told her. "This lady saw it!"

"You saw no such thing!" The manageress turned indignantly to Agnes and her companions. "There are no rats in here! We've certificates from the council!"

" Please calm yourself," said Miss Gillham placatingly. "You are quite correct. Nobody has seen a rat. At any rate, none that would require the attention of the Public Health Inspector. It is all a misunderstanding. But perhaps, if you will kindly find a box for our cakes, we will take our leave."

16

Stanley liked to go into a small yard outside his office in Victoria Hall, that bordered on Chapel Walk, and take a few puffs on his pipe. The women who shared the office with him insisted that they did not mind the tobacco smell, so really this ritual was an excuse to get away by himself and have some thinking space. A wall partially divided this yard from the Walk and Stanley stood behind it, concealed from passers-by, who could only see the smoke.

It must have been the smoke that on this particular morning announced his presence to the two people who pushed open the unlocked gate and entered the yard uninvited: a woman pushing a man in a wheelchair. They were beggars, or so Stanley assumed. He had seen them before, at the front of the building, shaking a tin at pedestrians and motorists parked on the street.

Stanley had a strict policy on beggars. In his youth, at theological college, he had been advised not to give them money, since it would probably be spent on drink. They could be given food, if any were available, and, unless disabled or infirm, should always be admonished on the need to find work.

In his older and wiser age, Stanley had dispensed with the moral lectures. He was well aware that work was not always available and even if it were, there were many causes other than simple laziness that prevented a person from holding down a job. But he stuck rigidly to the "no money" principle. If there happened to be a bunfight going on at the Centre, which was frequently the case, the supplicant would be directed to the kitchen door.

On this occasion, annoyed at the interruption to his peace, Stanley prepared to send one of the women for small packs of biscuits and some temperance leaflets; but then he recognised the man in the wheelchair.

Hubert had put on considerable weight, though he had never been slim. His hair was thinner and greyer. The left side of his body appeared to be immobile, though this did not apply to his face. His smug expression, Stanley thought, had not changed. The big difference was, that this Hubert did not speak. The old Hubert would have wasted no time in turning on the charm, bombarding Stanley with silver-tongued false apologies and excuses in the attempt to re-ingratiate himself.

"Dad had a stroke," explained the woman, reading Stanley's thoughts. "He struggles with his speech." She was in her forties, with brown, pulled-back hair that looked unwashed, and a reddish, pimpled face. Her jeans were worn and her sweater had a hole. But she spoke like the alumna of an expensive private school, and with the same confidence. "Do excuse us for butting in on you, Reverend Bolton. I'm Rosamund Scully. You're well acquainted with my father, of course."

"I am that," agreed Stanley shortly. He looked from one to the other of them, and could see no family resemblance.

"Did you get my letter?" continued Rosamund.

"I did."

"We've had no reply. I'm sure you must be very busy, of course."

"I did not deem that letter worthy of a reply, Miss Scully. Your father took the hard-earned money of our generous congregation and squandered it on materials for a building he hardly began, never mind finished, before absconding with what was left of the funds. You surely cannot imagine that after that he could have any claim at all on Methodist Homes accommodation.
And *I* cannot imagine where you got the nerve to ask such a thing."

"There is a clause," replied Rosamund calmly, "in one of the original documents, which states that all those who contributed to the building of the Cottages should have a claim on the accommodation, should they ever come to need it. My father built the foundations, which are still in place, are they not?"

"I cannot discuss this further with you, madam. You must excuse me." Stanley turned on his heel.

"We have a case!"Rosamund called after him. "You'll be hearing more of this!"

From the front window of his office, Stanley saw the two of them importuning the ladies who were arriving for their lunchtime meeting, Hubert shaking a tin at them with his good arm.

17

" You think it was the people, Priscilla, people coming to the door, that upset Agnes?"

Miss Gillham, now addressed as Priscilla, and Janet were drinking coffee in Nell's Cottage, having called on her on the way back from a shopping trip.

"I am sure of it. I had a good view of them, you see: a man in a wheelchair, and a woman pushing him. I think they intended to come in, but saw that *my* wheelchair was taking up space in the alcove, and thought better of it. Agnes recognised them- or one of them, anyway- and became distressed."

"And the "rat" was the man – or the woman?"

"Oh, the man, I imagine."

"In that case, I think I can guess who he is. Not his name, but what he did, I mean."

"And I think I have seen them again," said Janet. "Yesterday, when I went to my lunch club, they were begging outside Victoria Hall."

"Begging?"

"Shaking a tin at people. I only caught a glimpse of them in the tearoom, but I'm sure it was the same people."

"It's odd," observed Priscilla, "that they need to beg, and yet were apparently planning to visit a rather expensive tearoom. But perhaps," she added thoughtfully ,"there is a consistency to it. You say you know what the man did, Nell. Did it involve taking other people's money?"

" Well, yes, it could have done," said Nell. "I think the rat- the man in the wheelchair- was some kind of suitor who let Agnes down. Left her for someone else, maybe. I think there was money involved." She recounted the tale of the "rat bite" that had made Agnes ill, caused her to lose her job and, presumably, her bijou cottage by the sea.

"And she never got over it," said Janet. "She can't have got over it, if it upsets her that much seeing him again."

"I am worried about her," said Nell. "I haven't heard a word from her since last week. Jo says she's cancelled the sing-along on Wednesday."

"You'll see her on Friday though, won't you, Nell? Isn't that the day she comes to help you?" asked Priscilla.

"It is, but we have a rehearsal before then. If she doesn't come to that-"

"We could manage without her," said Janet. "We can practise our lines, without the songs. Come to that, Miss Gill-Priscilla- plays the piano."

"I am rusty," said Priscilla, "very rusty."

Nell tried to imagine Priscilla Gillham playing: "Oh I do like to be beside the seaside", and found it difficult. Besides, one missed rehearsal could set her co-producer on the slippery slope to dropping out altogether. " But Agnes has the book with the songs in," she said. "Friday is too long to wait. We'll go and see her," she decided. "Janet and I will go."

Priscilla frowned. Nell could be imperious at times. "I think perhaps, Nell, one should *ask* Janet if that would be convenient to her."

"Oh, I'm sure Janet won't -"began Nell, but tailed off, abashed at the reproach, and a little offended.

"It's all right." Janet came to the rescue. She had no liking for Agnes, but her sense of obligation to help those in need was strong. "I'll go with Nell," she said. "I agree Agnes shouldn't be left. We don't know what state of mind she's in.We'd better phone first though, in case she's out."

"Agnes doesn't have a phone. If she's out, we'll leave a note, and she can tell us when to come back," said Nell.

"In that case, I think Janet should go alone. No point in her picking you up Nell, if it's going to be a wasted journey. Janet can go alone and either speak to Agnes about a time you can both visit, or leave a note for her to get back to you about it." Priscilla Gillham could be officious too, when it came to protecting her friend from being put upon.

18

Hubert Scully had very little memory of his life before his family moved to the farm, but one incident from before that time had always been clear in his mind.

He was standing on a pouffe to see out of a front parlour window, peering through dirty net curtains. On the street stood two black horses, harnessed to a black carriage in which lay a long wooden box.

"What's in the box?" asked Hubert, addressing the thin, stooping, black-clad old woman who stood behind him. He thought of her as "the lady in black,"even later, when he understood she was his grandmother.

"A black cat," she answered.

"Can it breathe in the box?"

"It doesn't need to breathe. It's dead."

Upstairs, the baby mewled and began to cry. The old woman sighed.

Hubert remembered the night the baby had come. It was the night his mother had disappeared. He and his brother and sister had been asleep, but had been woken by frightening noises: heavy, hurrying footsteps, shouting, screams and crying. They had tried to go and find their mother, but the bedroom door had been locked. No-one had come when they had banged and shouted. They had hidden under the bedclothes, blocking their ears, till the noises had stopped, and they had fallen back to sleep. In the morning, Hubert had found the Lady in Black toasting crumpets by the kitchen fire, and, seated in a chair opposite her, a neighbour nursing a tiny baby with a bottle. At first, Hubert had been fascinated by the bottle: he had never seen a baby fed like this before. But he wondered why the neighbour had chosen their fireside to sit and feed her baby.

Later, he was told that this baby was his new little sister. This he did not believe. The baby, fed erratically on indigestible cows' milk, was colicky and fractious. Hubert wanted nothing to do with it. He was also told that his mother was poorly and had gone to the hospital to get better; but as the days went by and she did not come back, he was not sure about this either.

Hubert stared at the black plumes of the horses, blowing in the wind."Where's Mammy?" he asked the old woman.

She did not reply. Instead she went into the hall, where Hubert's father stood sobbing, and told her son to "be a man." A few minutes later, Hubert saw his father leave the house and join his uncles to walk behind the carriage. As it pulled away, four-year-old Hubert formed the impression that his mother had turned into a black cat, and was never coming back.

The farm Hubert remembered well: the drafty, unmodernised farmhouse and tumble-down outbuildings, bitterly cold in winter, battered with other kinds of weather most of the rest of the year. His father, trained as a gas-fitter, knew nothing about farming . His stepmother, whose inheritance it was, knew a lot, but was worn out by a series of miscarriages and stillbirths, and disheartened by her inability to bring a live child into the world. Getting up at five on icy mornings to muck out the pig and fetch in water from the pump before trudging through the snow to see if the school bus had managed to reach their isolated hamlet, Hubert made a decision: when he grew up, he was going to be rich.

He was helped in this ambition by being clever, and winning a scholarship to the Methodist Grammar School. His father, surprisingly (for he had never previously shown his younger son any preference), took some trouble to support Hubert in his studies. He succeeded in getting a charitable grant that enabled Hubert to board at the school, so that when he himself became ill, it was his older son, Desmond, who bore the brunt of the farmwork.

Hubert was overjoyed to escape the toil of the farm. He had no compunction over leaving his family, except, perhaps, for Alice, his older sister, who sometimes showed him sympathy. He was relieved to escape the others: his bullying older brother, his exacting father, his depressive stepmother and his resented younger sister, Lily, named for their mother and responsible, in his mind, for her death.

At school, the other boys despised him for his second-hand uniform and his ingratiating ways with the masters. Hubert taught himself not to care, by finding a way to get back at his schoolmates;:a satisfying way, because they had no idea he was doing it. He took to stealing tidbits from their tuckboxes, in tiny amounts, so no-one would notice anything missing: two toffees from a large bag, some broken bits of biscuit from the bottom of a box, a piece of icing or some cherries from a cake. Another child might have cried under the bedclothes at night: Hubert sucked and chewed silently.

He moved on from food to coins: a couple of farthings or a halfpenny here and there from change left in coat pockets. Hubert's charming manners and ostensibly impeccable behaviour made the teachers trust him. He was usually asked by the form teacher, for example, to take the weekly school fund money brought in by the day boys to the office, and as the teacher had not bothered to count it, this was a perfect opportunity to abstract a couple of sixpences. Hubert took his ill-gotten gains home with him for the holidays.

He knew exactly what he was going to do with the money. World War I was on, and German submarines were threatening British merchant ships. Sugar was rationed, but Hubert had noticed that the local village shop somehow managed to have a good supply of various sweets that was lacking in other places. He walked the three miles from the farm to the village and purchased the shop's entire stock of giant humbugs and gobstoppers. These, with great self-control, he stashed under the floorboards, only allowing himself to eat one.

On the first day back at school, Hubert held an auction in the playground. The sweets he had bought at four for a penny fetched an average of threepence each. Two boys struggled to outbid each other for the last one, which fetched a whole shiny shilling: all the money the bidder had on him. The winner whooped with glee; the boy who had been outbidden dissolved into angry tears.

Hubert slunk away to gloat alone. Under the bedclothes that night, savouring his triumph, he realised he had learned an important life-lesson: if people wanted something enough, they would pay anything for it. All you had to do was make them want it.

He worked hard at mathematics, which he saw as his way into the world of finance, and at sixteen was apprenticed to a firm of accountants in London. By twenty-three he had qualified as a chartered accountant, and was given more and more responsibility in investing in stocks and shares on behalf of the company. He was the apple of the boss's eye, and married the boss's daughter : a pretty, naïve eighteen-year-old named Belinda, who fell for his charms.

Though a self-centred husband, Hubert never intended to be an unkind one. But he found, rather to his own surprise, that he became jealous when Belinda talked to other men. He worried that her female friends encouraged her to go with them to places where these other men might be found, and also to drain away his money on expensive shopping trips. He took to restricting her housekeeping money severely, and sometimes locked her shoes in the wardrobe to make sure she got into no bad company while he was out. When Belinda ran away with a chimney sweep, Hubert was relieved that she had no access to his bank account, and therefore no access to his money, nor to the remains of the lump sum her father had given them both on their marriage.

Belinda's father however, unreasonably in Hubert's view, since she was the "guilty party", took his daughter's side in the affair. He had begun to become uncomfortable with some of Hubert's business deals; the shoes in the wardrobe were the last straw. Hubert lost his job.

Hubert did not allow himself to be dismayed. Like the proverbial door that is said to presemt itself when another closes, a new career prospect opened in front of his eyes. The “marriage market” was not called a “market” for nothing.

19

Agnes heard her doorbell ring and went to her front window. She peered down but could not quite see who stood on the chipped and faded tiles of the once stylish entrance to this decaying Victorian villa; but then the caller took a few paces backwards and looked up at Agnes's window. Agnes moved quickly away.

It was Janet. *So they had come looking for her, nosy beggars, wanting to pry into her private affairs.* Nell was probably worrying that she would not show up for the rehearsal on Thursday: well, that was Nell's problem. The whole idea of putting on a "musical play" with a cast of geriatrics was a ridiculous one anyway. The bell rang again.

Agnes moved to her side window, to stare out of that. It was what she had been doing most of the day. Seeing Hubert again had done this to her: she could concentrate on nothing. She had gone to the shops and come back without most of what she needed: she had not been able to think what to buy. Even making a cup of coffee took several attempts; she forgot what she was doing halfway through. It was absurd,that Hubert could still have this effect, after so many years. She would not think about him, she would not.

But the only subject of her thoughts, as she sat by the window, gazing absently at the neighbour, Ted, tinkering with one of his cars, was of course, Hubert: Hubert as he had been when they married, not young, but handsome, smart and vigorous; sometimes Hubert in the wheelchair, overweight and perhaps partially paralysed: still the same Hubert, who had seen and recognised her. Who was the woman pushing the wheelchair? Yet another wife? Or just his carer? A paid nurse? Logically, Agnes told herself, there was no reason why she should care. Just because she had had a chance encounter with the Rat who had wrecked her life, it did not mean she had to have anything to do with him ever again. It did not mean that she had to descend into illness again . She would not do that, she was not going to allow that to happen. That was why she could not meet Nell and the others, who had witnessed her weakness. She must be strong. She must stop this nonsense of sitting around, moping, unable to do everyday tasks..Matron would have whacked her round the head for such behaviour, and she would have deserved it. “If you can’t deal with all your problems, deal with the ones you can,” someone had once said to her:she couldn’t remember who, or why. But suddenly, Agnes got up and slipped on her shoes. She fumbled in her bag for some coins.

She hurried down the three flights of stairs. There was a pay-phone in hall of the building, but Agnes preferred the privacy of the box by the Post Office. She went out by the back door, not seeing the note from Nell that Janet had pushed through the front-door letterbox. She was about to fetch her bike from the shed when, above the noise of Ted’s revving engine, she heard yowling. Ted’s cat, a flea-ridden tortoiseshell that occasionally hissed at Agnes from the safety of the shed roof, was hanging by its collar from the wire-mesh fence, about to be strangled by the weight of its own body. Agnes grabbed its hindquarters and lifted it up to the level of the collar, and shouted for Ted. Oblivious, he did not hear her above the engine noise. Taking the whole weight of the struggling cat in one arm, and cursing its heaviness, Agnes, with her other hand, managed to undo the buckle and pull the collar off. Ted, having turned his engine off, noticed a woman-wasn't it that grumpy old bat next door? holding his cat, and was just in time to witness the collar coming off, the cat wriggling violently out of Agnes's grip, and leaping to the floor, scratching Agnes's hand on the way.

Agnes held up the collar. "Caught on the fence. Your cat was being strangled."

"Thanks,"said Ted, who was a man of few words. "I mean, really. I owe you a..." He had been going to say "drink" but thought better of it. Wasn't she a methodist or something? " ...a bunch of flowers. I hope your hand's ok. Here, wrap this round it." He offered her an oil-stained handkerchief, which Agnes declined.

She cycled to the telephone box, dripping blood onto the handlebars.

20

"Reverend Bolton, ladies and gentlemen," began Nell, "as you all know, we are meeting here to discuss our annual outing, which has unfortunately had to be postponed for the time being. As chairwoman-"

"I thought, " said Eric, "we was having a rehearsal, not a committee meeting".

"It *is* a rehearsal, Eric, *and* a committee meeting. We're rehearsing a play about a committee meeting."

"Well, Reverend Bolton isn't here."

"We're imagining he's here,"explained Nell. "Hopefully, he'll be here next time. I'm going to say his lines for him." Nell hastened on. "Now, Alf, it's your line next. When I say, 'as chairwoman', you interrupt me with…"

"*Char*woman!" said Alf. "Did you say *charwoman* ? I need me mantelpiece dusting, and a good sweep under t'bed."

Nell smiled and nodded. "As *chair*woman," she continued, "I have drawn up an agenda, which you will see in front of you. No," she told Eric, noticing that he was looking around him anxiously,"you won't *actually see it.* You can keep your script on the table, and pretend-"

"Like this," explained Bert, "then us can look at t'words when we're stuck."

Which will be most of the time, thought Nell. She could not imagine any of her cast actually learning their words, except possibly Priscilla and Janet, who were concientious. This was why she had written a sketch that could be enacted round a table, with papers in front of them.

"Why do we need an agenda," asked Gladys, "when we're only discussing where to go?"

"That's not on your script," said Bert. "We've got to stick to t'script."

"Oh," said Gladys. "Ooh, I'd love a seaside outing! We had lovely trips to Scarborough when I were a kid. Paddling in t'sea, eating winkles with a pin, donkey rides.

. This *was* on the script, and was supposed to be followed by "murmurs of agreement from several other committee members". Not hearing any, Gladys looked round impatiently. "Come on then, all of you! I don't call that 'murmuring in agreement.'"

"That's not in the-"began Bert.

"Script? I know it's not. But murmuring is, and nobody's doing it."

Priscilla and Janet obligingly murmured agreement.

" That's better.Thank you," said Gladys (unscripted.) "It's you now, Eric."

"Me?"

"Yes, with: "We used to go witht'Working Men's Club….'

"It would be better,"said Nell, "if we all just said our own lines from the script. If somebody's forgotten their turn, just give them a nudge or something."

“Yes, indeed!” Priscilla Gillham sounded authoritative. “Listen to Nell, everyone. Only say what’s in the script, or we shall never get through.”

“Thank you, Priscilla,” said Nell, unsure whether she was genuinely grateful or resentful at her own authority being usurped. Either way, the intervention worked. Chatting and superfluous comments ceased: the cast read through to the end of the script.

“We’ll put the songs in next time,” said Nell, as her players prepared to depart, “when Agnes is here.” ***If*** *she is here*, she added privately. She had seen and heard nothing of Agnes since the trip to the Lavender Tea Room, and it was now nearly a week since Janet had left the note. Agnes had missed this rehearsal *and* the previous one. “And I’ll see if I can get Matron and Dr. O along, if they’re not too busy.” Matron had sportingly agreed to play herself in the sketch, but Dr. O was still to be persuaded.

To Priscilla and Janet, who had recently joined them, she said: “Should we try another note to Agnes? Or just call round and see if she’s there this time?”

“I’ve a feeling she was there last time,” said Janet, “but didn’t want to let me in.”

“She never replied to my note,”sighed Nell.“ Do you suppose we’ve upset her?”

“I can’t think why. We’ve done nothing to cause offence. If she chooses to go into a sulk and not see us, there’s nothing we can do, is there?” Janet looked at Priscilla, to whom she always turned as a reliable source of wisdom.

"If you and I were more mobile, Nell, " said that lady, "it would be easier to know what to do. We cannot expect Janet to run about, as it were, after Agnes, if Agnes is unwilling to respond. But it is possible, of course, that she has not responded because she is ill, or in some kind of trouble. I am wondering if there is anyone else we could contact: a friend, a neighbour perhaps…maybe your brother-in-law. Well, I shall say goodbye now. I must go and have my rest." She wheeled herself away.

Nell and Janet went into the entrance hall, where a shabbily-dressed woman in her forties was telling Joanna, the Matron, in a strident voice: "Yes, but what I want you to do is tell me some dates and times when he *will* be here, so that I can come back then."

"Reverend Bolton doesn't have an office here," replied Matron. "His office is at Victoria Hall. You must make an appointment there if you want to see him. Now, if you will excuse me, I need to get on."

As they went out through the front door, Janet said quietly to Nell: "It's the woman I saw begging, with the man in the wheelchair."

"The Rat?"

Janet nodded. "They were at the tearoom, but didn't come in. I'm sure it's her."

Nell looked back and saw that the woman had come out of the building and was hovering, looking disgruntled. She set off across the grass, in the direction of the Cottages. Nell and Janet turned in the same direction, but walked slowly, at Nell's pace, and kept to the path. It led past the Cottages to the carpark.

"I wonder why she wants to see Stanley," said Nell.

"And why is she snooping about here?" added Janet. "I hope those two aren't causing trouble."

At the carpark, they said goodbye and Nell made her slow way back to her Cottage. It was untidy inside, and the sink was full of dirty dishes from breakfast and lunch. Nell would have to tidy up at least a bit before tomorrow, when the cleaner was due to come. Otherwise there would be complaints about her to the office again. She picked up the sherry bottle, noting that there was no more than half an inch left, and sighed.

The doorbell rang. "Coming!" she called, and limped back across the room to open it. To her astonishment, there stood the woman Janet had described as a beggar, companion of the Rat. Nell's heart missed a few beats, but the woman smiled politely and said in a refined voice: " I am *so* sorry to disturb you. Please don't be alarmed. I saw you going into your Cottage and I just wanted to – well, I'm interested in the Cottages, you see, and I would really like to talk to somebody who lives in one. My father helped to build them, you know, which means he's legally entitled to have one. If one becomes vacant of course. And, if he qualifies as being in need, which he does. He's disabled, after a stroke some years ago, but he had a successful building company once. Do you know of any Cottages likely to become vacant?"

"I don't,"said Nell. There was only George, at the end of the row, who might have to go into the rest home if he couldn't look after himself; but in spite of his not knowing what day of the week it was, he seemed to manage perfectly well. She changed the subject. "If your father helped with the building early on, he must know Stanley. My brother-in-law, Reverend Bolton."

The woman looked surprised and pleased. "Of course he does! They go back a long way, those two. He was a pillar of the Methodist Church in Sheffield, my dad! Well, fancy that! I came here, well.. to look around, but also to try and contact Rev. Bolton, and I've bumped into his sister-in-law! I'm so very pleased to meet you." She beamed at Nell.

Nell's habit of hospitality and need for company overcame both her remaining anxiety and the embarrassment that even she felt at the current state of her apartment. "You'd better come in," she said. "I was just going to put the kettle on. You must excuse the mess. I've a friend who helps but-she's not been lately."

She moved a pile of magazines off a chair so that her visitor could sit down and went to fill the kettle. A packet of teacakes was open on the kitchen counter. She was hungry; so too, she thought, would her visitor be, if she was really a beggar. But Nell felt also very tired. She looked over at the younger woman. "You can toast us some tea cakes, if you like," she suggested. "I'll do the butter. What did you say your name was?"

"Rosamund, Rosamund Scully."

"I'm Nell."

" You look tired, Nell. Let me do the toasting and the tea. Sit down, please."

As they ate and drank, Rosamund discovered that Nell's cottage belonged to Rev. Bolton personally, and had previously belonged to his mother; that Nell's friend who usually came to help, but whom she had not seen for a week, was named Agnes, lived alone in a bedsit in the village, and was a retired postmistress.

Rosamund opened her eyes wide at this last piece of information, then realised why this old woman with the multi-coloured hair and beads had seemed vaguely familiar. She had been in the Lavender Tearoom with Agnes and another couple of old biddies, the afternoon Rosamund and Hubert had come to the door, seen them all and turned away. "Not Agnes Greystone ?"

"Yes! Do you know her?"

"She's my stepmother. Or ex-stepmother, if you want to be exact. My father's ex-wife."

Nell found this hard to take in. She was very tired after the rehearsal. She had had no idea that Agnes had ever been married. Now, it appeared that she must have been married: to the Rat!

"Not that I've actually ever met Agnes," confessed Rosamund. "Truth to tell Father and I were out of touch with each other for many years. We only met up again recently. It's a long story. I would love to meet Agnes though. Do you have her phone number?"

"She's not on the phone."

"Her address then?"

It crossed Nell's mind that Agnes might not want this information to be given out."I don't know her address, I'm afraid," she lied. "Agnes always comes here, you see. She's never told me where she lives."

Rosamund looked disbelieving, but said pleasantly: "Oh well, not to worry then. I expect you could help me with Rev. Bolton's number, though, or his home address?

Or do you only see your brother-in-law when he comes here?"

"People usually see him at Victoria Hall,"

"I've tried that. They refused me an appointment, can you believe?"

"Oh dear, I am sorry-"began Nell uncomfortably, "but I can't -that is, he doesn't like his address to be made public. He's a busy man, it wouldn't do for people to be calling him at odd times of the day or night. You understand that, I'm sure."

"Well, of course, if you think *I'm* just another member of the *public*." There was an edge to Rosamund's voice. "I had begun to think we were *friends."*

It suddenly seemed imperative to Nell to get the daughter of the Rat out of her home. "You'll have to excuse me, Rosamund, I- I'm really tired, I think I shall have to go to bed."

She was worried that her visitor might refuse to leave, but Rosamund got up and made her way to the door. She said coldly: "I shall be in touch with Rev. Bolton one way or another, you know. My father has a legal right to one of these Cottages. More right than people like you, who clearly can't look after them properly."

When she had gone, Nell sank into a chair. She was shaking. She thought: *What a horrible woman. Is she really a beggar?* She could imagine Rosamund begging, importuning people till they gave her money. Her clothes were poor, her hair uncared for. She was definitely not *soignée.* Yet she was clearly an educated woman who had once been taught some manners.

21

Agnes found the letter on the hall doormat.The address was typed, but it was clearly not an official letter: the envelope was cheap and smelled of smoke. She recognised some misaligned letters from Nell's aged typewriter.

She took the letter upstairs and put it with the still unopened note from Nell that Janet had brought the previous week, which she had not found till some days later. She would open them if and when she was ready.

In the last day or so, Agnes had begun to feel a little better. She had taken some steps to improve her financial situation, and these had given her some hope. Nell's offer to ask her solicitor nephew to "write a letter" concerning her Post Office pension had made her wonder if she could employ a solicitor of her own, and a visit to the Citizen's Advice Bureau had confirmed that she was eligible for legal aid. The prospect of being able to help herself in this way had given her some confidence and taken her mind off the Rat. She shrank from opening the letters in case thay mentioned the afternoon at the Lavender Tearoom and refocused her attention on what she was trying to get out of her head at all costs.

Besides, she had broken her usual habit of keeping herself to herself in getting involved with Nell and her friends, and she felt it had been a mistake. On the other hand, she missed Nell's friendly acceptance of her, the generous supply of sherry and cigarettes.

She made an instant coffee and, to stop herself smoking, helped herself to two digestive biscuits. (She had to make her supply of cigarettes stretch without Nell's to supplement it.) She settled in the armchair, selected a new library book from her small pile, and began to read. It was a travel book, about a woman going round the world on a bicycle. Agnes had been looking forward to it.Ten minutes later, she had read two pages. She put the book down with a sigh. Those damned letters, opened or not, were not going to let her get the Lavender Tearoom and the Rat out of her head. Dammit, she would open them anyway.

The first one was simply a note from Nell saying she was sorry Agnes had been taken poorly in the café, hoped she was better, and wondered if she, Nell, and Janet could call round. The second read as follows:

Dear Agnes,

I do hope you are feeling better.We have been worried about you. I am writing because I think I should tell you about a visitor I had yesterday. It was Rosamund Scully, your stepdaughter....

Agnes's heart skipped a beat.

.....She came to the Cherry Trees looking for my brother-in-law, but Stanley doesn't have an office here and Matron said she'd have to go to Victoria Hall. Anyway, Rosamund came knocking on my door later-she saw me going in, and wanted to ask about the Cottages. She told me her father used to have a building firm, and built the foundations, but I expect you know all that. She was very surprised when I said I knew you. Wanted me to give her your address, but I didn't, because I wasn't sure

you'd want to see her-I think it was she and her father who came to the Lavender Café, wasn't it?I hope I'm not speaking out of turn – she's your family, Agnes, I know – but I didn't think she was a very nice woman. I hope I did the right thing...

We did miss you at the rehearsals. We did our best, but we really do need you!

Please do come and see me if you feel up to it. If you want to bring a bottle of sherry, I'll reimburse you....

Agnes was disorientated. *A stepdaughter who wanted to see her? Hubert was a liar and dissembler of the first order, she knew that, and his life had been full of secrets kept from her and others, but she had never come across the smallest hint, or ever had the slightest suspicion, that he had a child.*

Agnes made a decision. Avoiding Hubert and denying the past only meant they would haunt her for ever. Well then, she would take the bull by the horns. Instead of avoiding Hubert, she would confront him.

22

"Oh, Agnes! Thank goodness!" Agnes stood dripping on her friend's doorstep; she had got caught in the rain on her bicycle.

"We've been worried about you." Nell took Agnes's wet anorak and hung it over the back of an armchair.

"It won't dry there," snapped Agnes. "It'll just make the chair wet." She removed it and took it to the bathroom, to hang over the heated towel rail. She felt angry with Nell, without exactly knowing why, and hesitated before taking the sherry bottle out of her bag. But she had brought it because she really needed a drink herself, and she wanted the cost reimbursed.

Nell brightened at the sight of it. "I'll fetch some glasses."

Over the drinks, Agnes grilled her about Rosamund. Nell explained that Rosamund had seemed nice at first, but had then been nasty to Nell personally when she refused to give the contact details she wanted. "I've spoken to Stanley about it,"she continued, "and Doris. Stanley said she'd written to him, asking for a Cottage for her father. He said it was an outrageous cheek that they dared ask such a thing, they haven't got a leg to stand on. Hubert did start building the Cottages all those years ago, but didn't finish, apparently, just did the foundations, then ran off with the money. That is to say, there wasn't any money. He'd spent it on other things."

"I know. I was married to him."

Nell had temporarily forgotten that this must have been the case and looked anxiously at Agnes. "I'm sorry, I didn't mean…"

"Oh, there's nothing new you can tell me about Hubert's crimes, I assure you. He took the Methodist Home funds, and he emptied my bank account too, before I found out that our marriage was bigamous. I was very stupid. I paid it all into a joint account, and let him take over the mortgage on my seaside house.
There. Now you know exactly how big a fool I was."

"I'm so sorry," said Nell. "I'd no idea. No wonder you're upset, now he's come back."

" The bit I *didn't* know was that he had a daughter. Not that I care. She isn't my stepdaughter, anyhow. We were never legally married. And she sounds just as bad as him."

There was a silence: Nell was unsure what to say. Eventually she offered: "Stanley will deal with them. He says they've been begging, apparently, in a very intrusive way, outside Victoria Hall. They were bothering women going into the ladies' lunch last week, quite intimidating, Doris said. He's going to bring the police in if they don't stop it. It's not like they're homeless. The letters the daughter wrote had an address on, so I'm told."

"*Police,"* sniffed Agnes scornfully. "What good will the law do? Hubert got three months in prison for absconding with the building fund. *Three months!"*

Nell wanted to ask what he had got for the bigamy, but felt the subject was too sensitive.

Agnes answered the question anyway."He's never been punished for what he did to me. I've never told anyone what he did, except you." She paused. "Where did Doris say they lived?"

"Some flats, modern ones. By the station, I think she said."

23

Agnes stepped off the train at Sheffield station and made her way up the path towards Park Hill Flats. The August weather was warm, and it was quite a steep climb. Despite the cycling, she was overweight and far from fit. She stopped a couple of times and watched people going past her.

At the top, she approached a youngish woman with a pram and several children in tow, a woman nearer her own age lagging behind, carrying bags. "Excuse me, I'm looking for Hubert Scully and his daughter."

The younger woman looked blank, but turned and called: "Mum? Hubert Scully and his daughter?"

"They live here," explained Agnes, "but I've forgotten the number. He's in a wheelchair."

"Oh, aye, I know. Woman's got scraped back hair, wears old jeans. A bit scruffy."

Agnes nodded.

"They're just there, on t'end, ground floor. You have to go in that door, right along walkway, and it's first flat along. One with curtains drawn. They never open those."

"Thank you." Agnes found the flat easily; she had not expected it to be so easy, and now that she had no more to do than ring the doorbell, her mouth felt dry and her heart thumped. But having come this far, she was not going to be defeated.

She drew a deep breath, pulled her shoulders back, and her chin up, and, since there appeared to be no bell, hammered loudly on the door. It seemed someone was in: she could hear a television or radio.

Nothing happened for several seconds, then she heard slow, shuffling steps. The door opened half-way. Peering round it, breathing heavily, one hand on a walking frame, stood Hubert.

For a moment, he looked surprised and discomfited, and turned away; but he quickly regained his composure and said: "Well Agnes, I wasn't expecting this, but how lovely to see you!"

Agnes stared at the man who had once pretended to marry her. He was older, fatter, more stooped, his hair greyer and thinner. He was clearly disabled, but evidently able to walk, though with difficulty. His speech sounded weaker than she remembered it, but not impaired.

"I'll not say the same about you, Hubert. God knows, you're the last person on Earth I ever wanted to see again."

Hubert raised his eyebrows and smiled sardonically. "You won't want to come in then, I'm guessing."

"Is *she* here?"

"She?"

"Rosalind or whatever she calls herself. *Your daughter*."

"Rosamund. Not just now. She'll be back in an hour or so. We've got time for a catch-up. Old times sake? "

"*Old times!*"spat Agnes. "You seriously suppose I want to remember my times with you?"

He shrugged. "I'm betting you want to know about Rosamund, who *may* be my daughter. You'll need to come in for that. It's a long story, and I can't stand up much longer." He groaned slightly, with genuine pain.

"I just came to tell you.." began Agnes, but then wavered. She *did* want to know about Rosamund.

She followed Hubert's slow steps into a small living room. It was clean, but untidy. A television was on low in one corner. The painted walls were plain, the carpet of a faded, reddish-pink floral design. At one end of the rectangular room was a radiator with a shelf above, on which stood, at either end, two matching empty vases. In between lay several books, an alarm clock, an ashtray, and other bits and pieces. Above the shelf hung an old-fashioned, rather ornate , mirror, chipped at the edges.

Hubert settled himself carefully in a high-seated armchair. "Take a pew," he said to Agnes, indicating a black plastic sofa that stretched along the opposite wall. Agnes moved several pillows and a sleeping bag out of the way, and sat down.

"I can offer you a drink," said Hubert, "whiskey, gin, beer, but I know you don't drink that. Tea, coffee. I'd be a bit slow getting them, but feel free to help yourself. Make yourself at home, Agnes. We can be friends, can't we?" He gave her his wheedling, disarming smile, the smile that had charmed her all those years ago. It stirred something inside Agnes, a memory of feeling wanted, cherished. She felt her eyes prick with tears: it enraged her.

"I don't want your drinks, or your company, or anything to do with you or your beggarly daughter. Understand that, Hubert. You wrecked my life once. I've come here to tell you to stay out of it now, and keep your precious daughter out too. She's been tormenting my friend, did you know that? Stay away from me, and stay away from my friend, both of you!" Even as she shouted these words, Agnes realised they were hollow. She could not force Hubert and Rosamund stay out of her life; all she had done by coming here was expose her vulnerability. It had been a mistake.

"Rosamund is her own person," Hubert was saying. "I have no control over her at all, a poor old cripple like me. This is her flat," he continued. "She rents it from the council. She lets me live here, but she'll kick me out if I upset her too much, I know that. " He paused. "I can't manage on my own, as you can see. Rosamund looks after me. But the place is small for the two of us. Have a look, if you want. Only one bedroom, and there's not even a proper door on that. It opens off the hall. Tiny kitchen, tiny bathroom."

In spite of herself, Agnes got up and looked into the hall. "Where do you…?"

"I sleep in the bedroom. Rosamund has the sofa." He laughed. She doesn't look after me *that* well."

Agnes gave him a look of disgust. "I thought she was supposed to be your *daughter."*

Hubert spread his hands, palms up. "She *says* she's my daughter. It seems that when her mother, my first wife, ran off with her chimney sweep, she was expecting a baby. That baby being Rosamund.That's what Rosamund told me, anyhow. She may have been making up stories of course. Perhaps she didn't like being the daughter of a chimney sweep. Or perhaps she thought I was rich. She was wrong there, of course, if she did."

"Somebody must be registered on her birth certificate as the father."

"Oh, yes. that would be the sweep. But apparently her mother put him down because she didn't want to have anything at all to do with me again. I never knew Rosamund existed until..it must have been two and a half years ago. We met by chance in a hostel for the homeless. I'd just had the stroke. I'd recovered a bit, but not properly. Well, I never *did* recover *properly*. I've had bad times, you know, Agnes. Don't you feel just a little bit of sympathy.?"

Agnes stared at him, stony-faced. She gave a short, sarcastic, laugh. "Oh, we could *all* do with sympathy, Hubert. What makes you so special?" And yet, in spite of everything,inside, she *did* feel a small stirring of sympathy, at the thought of the stroke victim in the homeless hostel.

"Rosamund got herself this flat, somehow. She clever's like that, has her ways of getting round people. Perhaps she is a chip off the old block, after all!" he laughed. "She invited me to live here with her. So here we both are."

"And you live by begging."

"She's on benefits. She has mental health issues. I'm on benefits. We need to supplement our income. The begging was Rosamund's idea, by the way, I don't much care for it, but I do what I'm told, you see. I need to keep a roof over my head."

Agnes wondered what had happened to the money from the other women Hubert had bigamously "married". There had been at least one at the same time as herself, and probably others, before, after and during, probably wealthier than her. She knew he had run away to South America, or some such place. Presumably he had squandered the money on luxurious living there.

She said: "You have no shame."

For the first time in this conversation, Hubert lost his cool nonchalance. He said angrily: "Shame is for people who can afford the luxury of it. Life never gave me any advantages. I've had to take what I can. It's only what everybody does, when they're driven to it."

"You had parents! You had education!You had money that you stole from other people, mostly. You had advantages all right and wasted them all. So don't expect pity from me, Hubert Scully. You deserve to die in the gutter, like the rat that you are!"

Agnes had picked up her bag and was heading for the front door, when Hubert, who had remained silent during her tirade, said in a soft, wheedling voice:

"She doesn't look after me as well as you did, Agnes. Nobody's ever looked after me as well as you."

Agnes stopped and turned to face him. he smiled, the old beguiling smile. "Don't tell me you wouldn't want your piano back. Rosamund tells me you kept it at the Cottage while the old lady was alive, and could go and play it, any time. Back in storage, is it, now? Or did you have to sell it?"

"It's none of her business, or yours, where I keep my piano."

"I'm only thinking of you, Agnes. It must be terrible for you to be parted from it again. And Nell doesn't look after that lovely Cottage very well, does she? So

Rosamund says. Without you to help her, that is. Poor old thing, she probably can't help it. It must be too big for her anyway. Why does she need two bedrooms? She'd be fine with a smaller place, or a room in the rest home."

"You surely don't imagine anyone's going to give you and Rosamund Nell's flat?"

"Not *me!"* Hubert smiled. "Certainly not Rosamund! I'd be happy to send *her* packing. She's much too young, and I'm …undeserving, as you point out. But *you*, Agnes, they might give it to you! You're a little too young, of course, and able-bodied, but if you had someone to look after who wasn't – a husband, for example…"

Agnes stared at him.

"Think about it, Agnes, you and me with a nice little home, a bedroom each-I wouldn't impose- a garden. I know you'd love that.. I'm a free man now, you know, Agnes. Belinda did divorce me in the end, and the other marriages were never valid as you know. We could make it legal, this time. Sorry I can't get down on one knee.." He stopped. Agnes had left, slamming the front door.

24

Priscilla's room was on the second floor. She had to manoeuvre her wheelchair into the lift, and out again. She had left the door of her room propped open: it saved so much hassle when she came back. Once in the room, she could walk with her frame a few steps: enough to get from the bed to the chair, to the bathroom, to the window, where the view of the gardens was very pleasant. Unfortunately, she could not stand very long looking at it, and from the bed and the chair it was not visible. She had to content herself with looking at the sky.

She eased herself into her chair now, and set it into a reclining position, the back slanted, the footrest up. She lay back and studied the sky. In her teens, she had been always drawing, and had thought she might be an artist. It was her father who, realising she was never going to marry, had pushed her into a civil service career. Landscape-painting holidays were the closest she had come to her earlier ambition, and she remembered what a challenge it had been on those to capture the constantly changing interplay of light and colour of the sky.She thought of some of her pieces, hanging in her house. They were far from being masterpieces, but she was fond of them; Janet even more so. It had been Janet who had insisted on them being taken from the old house and hung in the new one- her "little" house, she called it- when she and Priscilla and her mother had moved. Now,

Janet lived alone in the little house, looking after it and the garden. Priscilla hoped that it was not too much for her old servant, that she was enjoying the freedom of the house, that she was not lonely. She worried that the little house was getting into disrepair, that if she, Priscilla, lived too long and became more helpless, it would have to be sold to pay for her care. Where would Janet go then?

Priscilla herself was accustomed to loneliness. She was well aware that people thought her stand-offish; they had done so all her life. But she did not despise the people around her, or consider herself superior: it was just that she rarely shared the same interests, and could not bear small talk. Also, she hated noise, and retreated to her room for quietness.

Until she had become disabled, activity had compensated for a lack of people in her life: a busy, demanding, sometimes fascinating career (though it had had it's tedious periods too); the painting, the rock-climbing. Now that these were taken away, what she enjoyed most was solving The Times cryptic crosswords in company with Janet, to whom she had introduced the techniques for tackling them some years ago. Priscilla had other interests, though, which she could not share with Janet or anyone else. A few years previously she had read books on quantum physics, and would have liked to discuss with scientists in that field their latest discoveries, and whether, for example, they had a bearing on theological questions concerning God and /or the nature of human consciousness. She subscribed to the

New Scientist, but, like most magazines, it dealt in bites and snippets of information.

Nell was a breath of fresh air for Priscilla: she was unlike anyone Priscilla had known before. She admired Nell's enthusiasm, her lack of inhibition in approaching others and involving them in her schemes. Nell made life just that bit more interesting. Janet thought so, too, Priscilla knew. But Janet did not like Agnes. Priscilla could understand why: the woman was a walking vinegar bottle. But Priscilla herself found Agnes's acerbity amusing rather than threatening. Was it misery or pique that was keeping Agnes away from rehearsals? She seemed somehow to have taken offence with the three of them, just because they had been in the tearoom and witnessed her distress. It would be a great shame if Agnes dropped out of the show: it would collapse, probably.

Unless you step in, she found herself thinking. She dozed off, dreaming she was playing "When I'm cleaning windows" on a grand piano at the Royal Academy of music, with Alf singing along.

25

"Ooh, I'd love a seaside outing! We had lovely trips to Scarborough when I were a kid. Paddling in t'sea, eating winkles with a pin, donkey rides…."

recited Gladys. She had worked hard, polishing her lines for the musical sketch. "Dabbling our feet in the sea, eating winkles with a pin, donkey rides."

"We used to go with t'Working Men's Club," said Eric on cue. He had been diligently learning his lines too. "Soon as we got there, me dad disappeared into t'pub. We'd no money for dinner-just a jam sandwich each, and I got a hiding for losing me boots in t'sea."

Alf took out an imaginary violin and hummed a mournful tune as he moved the imaginary bow over the strings.

"I think we're getting into this," said Gladys. "I think our musical sketch is going to be a bit of all right."

"It's more fun than watching t'box all day, anyhow," said Eric. "Things have livened up proper since Nell came."

"Aye, they have."

They were sitting in the drawing -room, waiting for Nell and Agnes to arrive.

The previous rehearsal had been in a side room, but Nell had insisted that they must have the piano for this one.

"Sketch'll be all right," said Bert, "as long as Agnes comes back to it. It'll be no good without music. Not that

I like the woman, mind. She's a right pain in the backside."

Gladys shushed him, because Nell had entered the room. Behind her came Priscilla, who manoeuvred her wheelchair up to the piano. Smiling, Nell announced that this lady would play a medley of sea-side songs, by way of introduction.

When Priscilla had finished, everyone clapped. Priscilla had got the best out of the slightly off-key instrument. Priscilla smiled and bowed slightly in acknowledgement. Then her expression changed to one of discomfort. Following her gaze, they all turned to see Agnes approaching from the doorway.
She regarded them coldly, hands on hips.

"Agnes!" said Nell. "just the person we need!"

"Clearly not," said Agnes. "Clearly I am surplus to requirements."

"Oh, no, Agnes! Of course not! Priscilla was just helping us while …"

"I can assure you, Agnes, I am only too happy to step down, now that you are here," said Priscilla.

Agnes sniffed. "But judging by the applause I heard just now, everyone else prefers you to me."

"Not 'alf we do,"said Alf. "Miss Gillham plays right gradely and she doesn't make a to-do about it neither." He received a kick from Gladys, whose foot went into paroxysms of pain.

Agnes looked, for a moment, as if she might burst into tears, but instead she said icily: "I'm glad you've made that clear, Alf. Thank you. Now I know where I stand. I should have known better than to expect any gratitude or appreciation. I have never received any, not for this sketch, nor for all the hard work I've put in here, over weeks and months."

"I'm sure we shall appreciate you *now*, Agnes," said Nell weakly, but Agnes turned on her heel and left, shouting over her shoulder: "I know when I'm not wanted!" Her exit was accompanied by Alf's slow clapping.

Everyone else was shocked into silence, until Priscilla broke it by saying stoically: "Shall I carry on, Nell, in the circumstances?"

Nell, who felt like crying herself, rallied her spirits and said gratefully: "Oh, yes please, Priscilla, if you would!" To everyone else she said, in as cheerful a voice as she could muster: "Right, we'll do this all the way through, songs and everything, with no more interruptions." And they did.

But later, when she was alone in her flat, a gloominess settled over Nell. She had run out of sherry, and there was no prospect of Agnes bringing her more. She sat in semi-darkness, getting cold but lacking the energy to fetch a wrap, or put on heat, or make herself food and drink, and ruminated sadly on the events of the day. She missed Agnes, in spite of feeling angry at the woman's unreasonable behaviour. Or had it been unreasonable? Perhaps she, Nell, had been at fault. Perhaps she had been wrong to bring Priscilla in.

The rehearsal had actually gone outstandingly well in the end, that was true. The more important characters had remembered their lines-they had obviously taken the trouble to learn them. Nell sensed a growing enthusiasm among her cast which had not been there before. Joanna had looked in and been impressed, and promised both to be at the next rehearsal, and to persuade Dr. O along too, if she could.

She felt lonely and depressed, missing so many people: her husband, Clive, dead before his time, her children, whom she seldom saw, her father, taken from her when she was only eight, her mother and aunts, and cousins, and her friends from London, who would probably never come and see her now.

Most of all, she missed her daughter, Imogen, and Imogen's children, who were growing up so fast, changing so quickly, when she had barely had a chance to get to know them. Imogen phoned Nell faithfully every Friday, but, if anything, the phone calls made Nell feel worse. Imogen seemed always tied up with and oppressed by the hard work of caring for small children, running a house and helping out on a farm.

A feeling of cold dread crept over Nell as she sat in the fading light. She was shivery, and there seemed to be a pain in her side. What if she was ill? Without Agnes's help, would she be able to continue to live here alone, to look after herself independently, never mind to produce a play, and make friends, and keep busy? *And if I can't do those things,* Nell told herself, *there will be nothing...*

If Nell had allowed herself to formulate this thought, it might have finished: *there will be nothing to distract me from the inevitable, from the fact that I am going to die.*

But she did not allow herself to formulate it. Instead she said, aloud: "There will be nothing to keep me going.

I must stop this, anyhow, it's doing me no good. She got up slowly and dragged herself to bed.

26

"The fact is, Mr. Bolton, your mother wanted me to have that Cottage. She more or less said that to me when I moved my piano in. She let me come and play it there, in her spare room, and she implied that when she was gone….."

" You've never mentioned this before, Miss Greystone. If you were so certain of what my mother wanted, why did you move the piano out when she died? Why did you not stake your claim then and there?"

"*I* was sure, in my own mind, that Hannah wanted me to have the flat. But …I didn't know if anyone *else* knew that. The flat wasn't mine, obviously. I couldn't leave my piano in someone else's flat, could I? Especially when…I thought it best to take it away until the will was sorted, until we knew whose flat it was, going to be, exactly."

"Did you think my mother was actually going to *leave* the flat to you, Miss Greystone?"

"Of course not!" But Agnes coloured as she said this, because she had once dared to hope that might be the case.

Stanley said kindly: "Look, Agnes, let's go into my office and sit down," for Agnes had accosted him in a corridor, and it was not very private.

Fortunately neither of his two assistants was present, and he offered Agnes one of their empty chairs, whilst taking the other himself, in order to avoid sitting officiously behind his desk. "Mother," he explained, "left me her Cottage, which she owned. She left it to me, and said specifically, in her will, that she wanted me to use it, that is, to rent it out, to somebody who was both in need of it, and deserving. This information is of course personal, I am not under any obligation to share it with you or anybody, but I choose to do so because I want to help you understand." Agnes started to say something, but he held up a hand. "Now I know, Agnes, that you are a most deserving person, you were a great help and support to my mother, as well as a good friend. I am also aware that she did indeed favour the idea of the Cottage going to you, though I have to state clearly that she never actually told me that in so many words, either in speech or writing. I think, probably, that was because she realised, as you must be aware yourself, that you are quite a bit younger and sounder of limb than the average occupant of our Cottages."

"Much good it does me! Perhaps I'd better fall down the stairs and make myself a bit less 'sound of limb,' had I? My baby grand piano is rotting away in storage- that never does them any good, you know-and I can never play it. Isn't that a disability? It is to me! It's worse than having my arms cut off!"

"Come now-" Stanley was on the point of giving a moral lecture on the dangers of ingratitude for one's God-given health and strength, but thought better of it. So desolate was the look on Agnes's face, he could almost believe her words were literally true. "It is a trial for you Agnes, I see that," he said, and did not add, as he might have done: "We must pray for strength, you know, to bear the slings and arrows of outrageous fortune."

Instead he said: "Obviously, if you *do* one day move into one of our apartments, which I am sure will be a strong possibility in a few years' time, my mother's one will be the most appropriate one for you. It's the only one with an extra room, with space for your piano. But as you know, it's occupied at present. There's no question of you having it yet awhile, you must see that."

"Nell can't look after it," said Agnes bluntly. "I mean, she can't look after herself in it. She doesn't eat properly, she doesn't wash up-or wash herself much, either, or her clothes-it's unhygienic. Her smoking's made a total mess of the carpet, and it's a fire hazard! It's only because I've been helping her these last several months that Nell's managed at all, and I was cutting off my nose to spite my face, wasn't I, because while I was helping her manage, she was able to stay in the Cottage, and I was stuck in a lousy bedsit on the top floor! Well, my help has come to an end, so we'll see how your sister-in-law manages now, Mr. Bolton, won't we?"

"Thank you, Miss Greystone, I'll make a note of everything you've said." The sympathy Stanley had felt earlier was fast ebbing away. He stood up and opened the door.

"Confound the woman," he muttered, when Agnes had gone. He would talk to Doris that evening. Somebody needed to do something about Nell.

Agnes left the building in a state of distraction, overwhelmed by her emotions. It was in this state that she was approached by a poorly dressed younger woman, with rough skin and scraped back hair. "Mrs. Scully!"

said the latter. "I think it's time we got to know each other. I'm your stepdaughter.I'm Rosamund."

"Your are *not* my stepdaughter." Agnes glared with indignation at the younger woman. "You *may* be Hubert's daughter, possibly. That I neither know nor care. But since I was never legally married to Hubert, or anybody else, I am *nobody's* stepmother."

"Fair enough," said Rosamund, unperturbed. "I was just trying to be friendly -to show that there is a link between us- because there *is*, isn't there? I mean, I'm his daughter, and you lived with him, *as* a wife. For a bit, anyway.I just thought we should get to know each other. We may be able to help each other. After all, we're both interested in the same apartment, aren't we? The Cottage?"

Later, at home, Stanley did not say anything to Doris about Agnes's visit. He was not sure that it would be ethical, and anyway, the episode was distasteful to him. But he decided a little probing around the subject might help him understand better what was going on. As they were eating their tea (dinner was a midday meal in the Bolton household) he said:"I had the impression Nell and Agnes Greystone were good friends. Surprising, I know, but they did seem to get on. Didn't you tell me Agnes was giving Nell a lot of help?"

"Oh, yes, they were friendly, all right. They were planning a concert together, if you remember. I think they asked you to be in it, didn't they?"

"For my sins, yes. Is it still going ahead?"

"As far as I know, yes, but Nell did mention that Agnes seems to have gone off in a bit of a huff. Stopped coming to rehearsals. Nell's not sure how to get her on side again."

"Would it be anything to do with her piano, do you think? She's not got a home for it now that Nell's in the Cottage, maybe that's put her nose out of joint."

"I've not heard anything like that, but Nell did say something about Agnes not coming to rehearsals, and then when she did come back, somebody else was playing the piano and she took umbrage. Nell's hoping it'll all blow over. Anyway," Doris added thoughtfully, "if Agnes is bothered about her piano, there might be a simple solution to that."

27

"*Agnes* sent you?" Nell looked dubiously at Rosamund, who was standing at her open door. She remembered the woman's unkind remarks the last time they had met.

"Yes. She's my stepmother, if you remember, well *honorary* stepmother, I suppose. You couldn't remember her address last time I saw you," added Rosamund sarcastically, "but we managed to meet up just the same. Agnes thought I might be able to fetch your pension for you and..do any bits of tidying up you might need. She's sorry that she hasn't been able to get here herself recently."

Nell did not like Rosamund, and was afraid of what she might demand, but an offer of help was an offer of help. Perhaps this was a peace-offering from Agnes. "I fetched my pension yesterday," she said. "I get it on a Tuesday."

"Well," said Rosamund. "Cigarettes? Sherry?" she lowered her voice slightly on the last word.

"Actually,"said Nell, "I'm running out of tea."

That conversation had taken place eight days previously. Nell had given Rosamund money from her pension, and Rosamund had come back with Nell's shopping, scrupulously producing the relevant till receipts. Nell had been grateful, and felt obliged to invite Rosamund in for tea. Rosamund had washed the dishes, cleaned the sink, and emptied the bin. She had produced a roll of plastic binliners, bought, as she took care to explain, at her own expense, and not out of Nell's money. "If we use these Nell," she explained, "it'll stop the tea leaves getting everywhere." Since then, similar visits had twice taken place. Both times, Rosamund had been pleasant and friendly, and had not made unkind remarks or fished for information. Nell had tried to get her to talk about Agnes, hoping the latter might have a message, but Rosamund was vague and seemed to have lost interest in her "honorary stepmother."

Now, Nell was sitting at the table, counting and recounting her money. She was sure there had been another ten-shilling note, which was missing. She knew she had not lost it. She always kept her pension money in the same place, on the sideboard. She took some of it to put in her purse if she was going to the shops or on a trip, but she had not been out since collecting her money the previous day, and the ten-shilling note was not in her purse. It was not on the floor. It had gone. And it was not the only money that had disappeared recently: a few days earlier, she had discovered that she had much less silver than she had thought. Nell realised with a shock that someone was stealing from her.

That morning, Rosamund had come to do Nell's shopping. Nell had given her two pound notes to cover it, and Rosamund had brought back the ten-shilling note as change, along with a half-crown and some coppers. Nell had taken the change from Rosamund and put it on the sideboard with the rest. Rosamund had only stayed another minute, saying she had to get back for an appointment, and Nell was sure that during that time her visitor had not gone near the sideboard. Nell was quite prepared to accept that Rosamund could be a thief, but the fact was, she had had no opportunity to take the money. No-one else had visited Nell, so that left one possibility: someone had come in while Nell was out and taken the cash. She had gone out soon after Rosamund had left, over to Cherry Trees to see Joanna about rehearsal arrangements. She had left the door unlocked, as she often did if she was not going out for long. She must stop that. Perhaps she should get in the habit of putting her money away, too, in a drawer somewhere, out of sight. Nell decided to report the matter to Alison in the office: if there was someone hanging about stealing money, other people should be warned. She took her stick, put her keys in her pocket, and made sure the door locked behind her before shuffling along the corridor to the office. Everything seemed an effort today, and this short walk made her breathless. A pain in her back and shoulder pulled her up short, and she had to wait for it to subside before moving on.

"Are you quite certain you *had* a ten-shilling note, Mrs. Bolton?" asked Alison, in a voice louder than necessary. Nell was not deaf.

"Quite certain-" began Nell. A ten-shilling note had a distinctive pinkish-brown colour, and she definitely remembered Rosamund handing her one. But a doubt suddenly struck her. Could that have been on a different day? No, it had been today, she was sure.

Alison noticed the hesitation. She looked sceptical. "And you say it happened twice?"

"Yes, last Friday I think it was. Or Thursday? I had a lot of silver, two half-crowns and some shillings, and when I went to put some in my purse, most of it had gone."

"You didn't say anything at the time."

"No. I thought maybe I'd miscounted it. Or spent it and forgotten, I don't know. But now it's happened again today, I'm worried there's a burglar about. I thought you should know, so you can warn the others. You could p'rhaps send a note round."

Alison smiled wanly. "Let's see how things go, shall we, Mrs. Bolton? You see, I wonder why the 'thief' only took a ten-shilling note and some silver. Why not take all the money?"

28

She was not a thief, Rosamund told herself, because she had not taken Nell's money for the sake of the money. If she *had* done it for the money, she would have taken the lot. No, she had done it for more complicated reasons than that, and complicated, in Rosamund's perverse and idiosyncratic line of reasoning, meant more worthy. It had been necessary to take the money as part of her scheme to get Nell out of the flat, and that was a worthy cause, because it meant that the man she had adopted as her father, who was disabled and who had a right to the accommodation he had helped to build, would have a better chance of getting it for himself. Any of the other Cottages might have done, but they were not available either, and besides, Nell's Cottage had an extra room: the room that had housed Agnes's piano, another connection with the family. At this point the plan in Rosamund's mind became a little fuzzy. The best outcome would be if her father could get the apartment, and Rosalind move in with him to look after him, perhaps with Agnes's help. They would rapidly discover he was too much for them to cope with and get him moved to the rest home. Agnes would stay in the Cottage, and would be grateful to Rosamund for helping her to acquire her home. Rosamund would convince the Methodist Homes board that she needed to live there too, to look after her increasingly ailing stepmother: ailing in what way, Rosamund had not decided: something to do with nerves, possibly? Nell had told Rosamund about the panic attack in the tearoom. And when Agnes sadly passed on -she was not a healthy woman, after all-well, they couldn't turn out the poor bereaved step-daughter straight away, could they? There would be time for Rosamund to work out a reason why she should stay-squatter's rights or something? She would worry about that later, cross her bridges when she came to them. The problem with the scheme was that Agnes had made it clear she would have nothing to do with Hubert; but what if Rosamund could persuade Agnes on the grounds that they would have Hubert off their hands before too long? After all, Agnes was entitled to some compensation for the way Hubert had treated her. Revenge, yes! She would help Agnes get her revenge, and Agnes would be her friend for life, or if not friend, her ally. Rosamund did not expect to have friends, but she needed allies. Everyone had to fight for what they could get in this eat-or-be-eaten world, and it was lonely without allies.

It had been easy to steal the money. The first time, she had simply slipped a few coins quietly into her pockets while Nell was busy making tea; the second, she had hidden in the bushes after saying goodbye to Nell, knowing that the latter would go out soon, and probably without locking the door, so that Rosamund could sneak back in and get the ten-shilling note. She would have liked a third go, but if money disappeared too often on days when Rosamund visited, even Nell would begin to suspect her. Then fate appeared to intervene and help her plan along.

On Wednesday morning, Rosamund arrived as usual to see if Nell wanted shopping. On her way in, as she passed the office, Mrs. Charnock was just coming out. Rosamund and the cleaner had not previously met, but Mrs. Charnock vaguely recognised the other and said, on a hunch: "Aren't you t'lady as visits Mrs. Bolton?"

"Yes. I'm just on my way there now."

Mrs. Charnock adopted a confidential tone. "Have you,"she said, "noticed anything about Mrs. Bolton lately?"

Rosamund looked interested but shook her head slightly.

"It's just that-when I went to do for her yesterday-she seemed -well, confused."

"Did she?"

"I knocked and she didn't answer, so I knocked again and went in. She

were 'alf asleep on t'settee. It must 'ave been me knock woke 'er up. She were a bit agitated, saying something about pies and gravy, and looking at me like she didn't know who I were. Then she said: 'Oh, Mrs. Charnock, sorry, I thought you were the policeman. I said 'what policemen?'and she said: I never told him about the money, did I?" Then she went back to sleep and dozed till I'd gone, even though I had t'hoover on."

"That's very concerning," said Rosamund, hiding her delight. "Thank you for telling me. Have you..?" She nodded toward the door of the office,

"Oh aye, I've told them in there," said Mrs. Charnock,"I thought they needed to know.And *they* said 'oh dear, she's been reporting money going missing recently, I wonder if she's going a bit …you know…' Poor old thing," finished Mrs, Charnock.

When she had gone, Rosamund knocked on the office door herself.

29

Doris found her sister-in-law on the sofa, covered by a rug. Clearly she had been asleep, woken by Doris's knock. This was surprising, as it was the usual time for Doris's fortnightly visit. "I'm sorry, Nell, I thought you were expecting me…"

"I was expecting you, of course. Just put my feet up, for a minute. Must have nodded off." She sat up, swung her legs onto the floor, and perched on the edge of the sofa, looking dazed.

"Nell," said Doris. "You're shivering."

"I am a bit chilly."

"It's warm in here. Stay there, I'll put the kettle on."

"No,"protested Nell, but as she got to her feet, she swayed and had to sit back down.

Doris felt Nell's forehead. "You're hot, Nell. You've a temperature. I'll go over to Cherry Trees, I've an an idea Dr. O's there, it's his time for visiting. And if he's not, they'll have to send for him. Don't you dare move an inch till I come back."

"I don't need…" began Nell feebly, but felt too exhausted to put up an argument.

Doris returned with the announcement that Dr. O would come over when his round at the rest home was finished. "And I told that Alison in the office you're not well. She said you'd reported some money missing. Nell, have you had that Rosamund round here?"

"She's been helping me. She said Agnes sent her."

"*Agnes* sent her?Did she indeed! I'll give her a piece of my mind! Stay away from Rosamund, Nell, she's a menace. I know that sounds nasty, but I've seen her begging outside Victoria Hall. She's quite threatening about it."

"She has said some very unkind things, it's true, but-I thought she really wanted to help. I won't let her in again." She added after a pause: "Do you think it was Rosamund took the money?"

"I think it very likely."

"Alison thought I'd imagined the whole thing. She thought I was going doolally, I could tell. And then Mrs. Charnock came in and woke me up and I think she thought the same thing. I was wandering a bit, I must have been dreaming." Nell sounded breathless, and winced as she spoke.

"It might have been the temperature," suggested Doris. "Happen you had it yesterday. You've not been well for a bit, have you Nell? You should have told me. Anyhow, I made it clear to Alison that you are *not* doolally. Mrs. Charnock had said something to her, I think. And Rosamund had told her about the missing money, which is odd, considering it was probably Rosamund who…" Doris tailed off, for it had just occurred to her why Rosamund might have reported thefts she herself had committed. "Well, I've done my best to set the record straight. But what was Agnes thinking of, sending that dreadful woman here? And to think I was going to ask you if you would be willing to keep her piano here for her, like our mother-in-law used to do!"

"Oh!" said Nell. "Well, of course, I'd be happy to keep the piano here! I'd just never thought of it, that's all. But not -well, I suppose, not if she's in cahoots with Rosamund. That does put it in a different light."

"You probably shouldn't talk if it hurts you, Nell. Just rest. Do you need extra cushions? I'll get you some aspirins. And tea of course."

Dr. O diagnosed pleurisy and prescribed bedrest and antibiotics. Both he and Doris wanted Nell to go into the nursing section of Cherry Trees, but she refused adamantly, and so, for the next few days, she lay in her bed at home, getting up only to shuffle cautiously to the bathroom with the aid of a walking frame Joanna had brought over. ("In case you feel faint," she had explained. "You don't want to fall over.") Her pension was tucked away out of sight, some under her pillow, some under the breadbin, so that her front door could be left unlocked for people to come in and check on her. Ruth, her neighbour, came, and sometimes Janet, and Doris came every day. Some of them brought her food, which she mostly did not eat, and made her cups of tea. Janet brought in a large vaccuum flask with a tap and set it up by the bed, as they were all worried about her getting up and lighting the gas and boiling kettles when they were not about.

She listened to the radio, and dozed, sometimes cheered by the kindness of her friends, by a phone call from her daughter and a rare letter from her son in Australia, by the hope that she would soon be back to normal. But at night, vivid dreams as well as painful breathing disturbed her sleep. Sometimes Agnes appeared in her dreams, a disgruntled Agnes whom Nell had somehow let down, without knowing exactly what she had done. In one dream she was a newlywed, with her handsome, clever husband and in their smart new home. Another time she was caring for a baby, a beautiful, bonny baby, her pride and joy. In the worst dream, a recurring one, she was with her mother in her childhood home, though she did not feel like a child, but seemed ageless. Her mother was cooking the evening meal; her father was expected home at any moment. Pervading all these dreams, especially the last, was a sense of impending doom. She would wake, coughing, in the early hours of the morning, and feel alone, anxious for the night to be over, for light and noise and company.

30

Doris knew where Agnes lived. At 9.15 the next morning she planted herself firmly on the threshold of Agnes's lodging house, taking care to stand as close to the front door as possible, so as not to be visible from an upstairs window, and rang Agnes's bell. She had just rung for the third time, with no obvious response, and was beginning to despair, when she heard footsteps approaching from within. A young man opened the door and stepped out, seemingly in a hurry. As he did so, Doris pushed past him into the hall. "Hey!" he called after her. "You can't just…" He looked back and saw that she was already on the stairs, and shrugged. He had a bus to catch.

"Miss Greystone! Agnes! I know you're in there! Open up!" Doris banged loudly on the door of the top-floor bedsit. A woman on the next floor down came out and stared up the stairwell at the disruptive visitor, and Doris felt her cheeks and neck flush. Stanley would be ashamed of her behaving as she was. Then the anger that she had felt when Nell had told her about the pension came back, and she banged more furiously.

Agnes, who had just been dressing when the knocking began, pulled a dressing gown over her petticoat, shuffled her feet into her slippers and went to open her door. Thinking it was probably some other resident, perhaps Elsie downstairs wanting to borrow a shilling for her meter or complaining about the stair cleaning rota, she shouted back grumpily: "No need to break the ruddy door down, is there?" She was astonished to find her visitor was the Methodist Superintendent's wife. "Mrs. Bolton! *Do* forgive me. With all that noise, you sounded like a fishwife!"

Doris ignored the insult, vaguely wondering why fishwives had such a reputation for verbal abusiveness. Her late, saintly mother-in-law would have had something to say about that, coming as she did from a long line of fisherfolk. "You'd better let me in, Agnes," she said calmly, "or I'll give you a piece of my mind out here."

31

Agnes thought of her old boss, Mr Chilton, God rest his soul, and wished he were with her now. He had taught his young protégé how to drive, and trusted her with the use of his van to fetch the stock with which he liked to boost his post office income: stationery, greeting cards and picture books from a supplier in Sheffield. Agnes had become a proficient driver before the driving test had become compulsory in 1934, and so had never had to take it. She had never owned a vehicle herself, however.

"It's all in working order." The owner of the camper van looked slightly offended at Agnes's hesitation. "Would you like a test drive?" Agnes swallowed. Hubert had had a car when they first "married", and she had sometimes driven it. But since then? "I'm a bit rusty," she said. "And I've never driven one of these before. My car was-er-smaller."

The man smiled. "I'll show you the ropes then. Climb in." Agnes stepped up into the passenger seat-*climb is the right word*, she thought, but she must not let this young man think it was a struggle for her. She had had enough patronage from young men recently. *That young man at Dodge, Fraud and Child, for example. (I must stop calling them that. One day I might say it in front of them.) Child didn't look a day over fifteen.*

In spite of Agnes's disparaging opinion of them, the solicitors at Hodge, Ford and Son, had done well for Agnes. The youthful one, whose name was not Child, or

Ford, or Hodge, but something like Carter, or Parker, (Agnes could not quite remember), had spent some hours studying her carefully kept pay slips, pension documents and letters and explained, across the ancient red-and-black-ink-stained table, that he thought there was some evidence that the Post Office had been responsible for some irregularities regarding sick-pay and National Insurance contributions that might affect her current pension.

Legal Aid was a wonderful thing: she could not have afforded the services of Child without it. He had worked indefatigably on her behalf, writing letters, arguing on the telephone, not taking no for an answer, until finally a cheque had arrived on the doormat of Agnes's lodging house. She was grateful, and she left for Child at the offices of Hodge, Ford and Son an enormous Cadbury's Selection Box with a thank you card and only a slight ironic intention.

By the same post in which the cheque arrived came a letter from her Canadian cousin, who had been travelling around the country in a dormobile, and sent photographs of blue lakes and rocky shores. They could hire one, she suggested, when Agnes came to visit. Agnes was far from sure she wanted to explore Canada in the company of this woman she had never met, but the dormobile was a different matter. Suddenly Agnes had known what to spend her money on.

All this had happened on the day that Doris had come banging on her door, accusing her of being in cahoots with her so-called daughter-in-law in some kind of plot against Nell. Agnes had not quite taken in the details of

Doris's accusation, being too incensed to listen properly, but she had expressed her outrage that Doris should think her capable of any such behaviour. Doris, on reflection, realised she had acted too quickly. She knew Agnes was not dishonest: vindictive, perhaps, yes, but not to the point of actually harming anybody. And Agnes's antipathy to Rosamund had struck Doris as genuine. Doris had apologised, and made her way down to the front door. Seeing the post on the mat, as a gesture of appeasement she had carried it up three floors to Agnes, who had received it without thanks.

Agnes had gone straight to the bank to pay the cheque in, her head spinning and her heart pounding with such a confusion of rage, triumph, excitement and defiance that she might have gone and bought a gleaming motorbike with caravan sidecar if the bank clerk had not reminded her that the cheque would take a few days to clear.

She had bought an Exchange and Mart instead, treated herself to a box of fondant fancies and sat down on a park bench to consider things. She felt suddenly extremely tired, and realised that what she wanted most of all was to share sherry and cigarettes with Nell. But Nell was ill! She suddenly remembered that Doris had mentioned that. And hadn't Doris also said that Nell would be happy to accommodate the piano?

The camper van seller jumped in beside her. "It's easier than a car," he said. "Honest. You get a fantastic view all round, see?" They drove around the block a couple of times, then Agnes inspected the inside of the van. There were a couple a of gas burners and a grill, a small sink for washing up, a portable toilet concealed under a seat, benches that converted to a bed. The cushions were shabby, the single curtain torn and coming off its runner. "It needs sprucing up a bit," conceded the owner, "But the engine's fine. It runs well." He explained with pride how he had converted it from a former ambulance.

"Humph,"Agnes sniffed. "A bit noisy if you ask me." She was afraid of being cheated, but realised she had no idea at all how to judge whether the van was value for money or not. "I'll need a day or two to think about it."

"Of course." The man nodded, but he did not promise to keep it for her. That was fair enough. He would have to sell if someone else came along and offered the full price. But all the way home Agnes found herself fervently hoping that he would not.

The next moment, she told herself she was being absurd. To buy an old van when she knew nothing of how to judge its condition was irresponsible. And where would she keep the thing? Could she, a single woman on her own, actually travel around the country in it? How safe would that be?

As she turned into her front path she was vaguely annoyed to see car parts
strewn across next door's drive, oil stains on the concrete, a strong smell of petrol pervading it all. The neighbour, Ted, was tinkering with one of his cars again. He looked up and nodded as Agnes went by. This had happened ever since Agnes had rescued his cat. He had been genuinely grateful for that, revised his opinion of

her as a moany old bat, and promised her a bunch of flowers, which he had then forgotten to buy. He did not exactly smile, that would have been over-familiar, and he did not speak. Ted was a man of few words, some would have said rude. But taciturnity was something Agnes understood, and it did not offend her. She returned the nod and approached her front door, then turned back. Why not ask a favour? He owed her a bunch of flowers after all. “Ted!”she called. “I need help!”

Ted had his head in the engine and jumped up in alarm.

“Advice, I mean,” explained Agnes. I need your advice.”

32

"Your lungs are improving, Mrs. Bolton. But you must stay off the cigarettes for a few days, to give them a chance." Dr. O had noticed, as he came in, a half-smoked cigarette, extinguished in an ashtray on the bedside table. Nell had hastily pushed the ashtray under the open page of a magazine.

The doctor removed the stethoscope from his ears and considered the best line to take. He could order Mrs. Bolton to stop smoking, on pain of death. In the unlikely event that she obeyed him, would that prolong her life? Probably a little, but not necessarily very long. The damage was already done. Would it make her life more comfortable? Yes, once she had overcome the cravings, but they would be hard to bear.

Nell, sitting on the edge of her bed, rebuttoned her dressing gown. "I haven't smoked much," she said defensively. "I haven't felt like it." There had also been a need to conserve her cigarette supply, since no-one had been willing to fetch them for her.

"None at all would be best for the next couple of days.....shall we say just today and tomorrow, including the nights. Can you do that? By then, you should be able to go out and about again, get on with this dramatic production we are all looking forward to. Matron has told me all about it."

"I'm hoping you're going to be in it, doctor. The next rehearsal's booked for Friday."

"Then you will need to be well for it. Here's a bargain. You stay off the cigarettes till Friday- that's two days, which is what I suggested-and rest, and I will come to your rehearsal."

"Done!" said Nell. "Here, you can look after them for me till then." She took from her dressing-gown pocket an almost full packet of twenty cigarettes, and, mastering a sinking feeling, handed it to him. They both knew, of course, that he would have no way of checking whether she had kept her part of the bargain, but he felt he had made an attempt, and she felt she would make one.

But Dr. O had not finished. "You must not forget, Mrs. Bolton, that you are mortal, like the rest of us."

Mortal. The word went through Nell like a jolt of lightening. "Mortal" was not a word she liked to hear, in relation to herself. This was not fair. This was not the kindly, humorous Dr. O she was accustomed to. She said testily: "Well, I know that."

"But you don't like to face the fact. Nobody does, of course, but it can be a mistake. I have had many patients who came to me too late. They ignored their symptoms, hoped they would go away. If they had just come earlier, their lives might have been saved, or prolonged, or at least made easier." Seeing his patient's frightened face, he sought to reassure her. "I am not suggesting that *you* have come too late, Mrs. Bolton. As I said, you should be up and about again very soon." He sat down on the bed a few feet away from her. "What I mean to say is, if one is very afraid of death, one may not be able to take necessary steps to remain healthy, because to do so would be to acknowledge one's mortality. Ironically, this attitude of fear may hasten the very event which is feared."

"I don't see how it helps to dwell on those things." Nell was on the verge of tears. The dream she had been having in the last few days was vividly present again: the policeman at the door. She shuddered. Death was a policeman at the door: sudden, cruel, and taking somebody out of your life. How could anybody enjoy their life if they let themselves think about that, if they were always thinking that that could happen? "It can be so sudden and cruel," she whispered. "Taking somebody who isn't even old. Somebody who's always been there, gone forever."

"You have lost someone close that way?"

"My father. Killed by a train when I was eight."

"I also lost my father." The doctor drew his hand across his neck in a gesture of throat-cutting.

Nell gasped.

"My mother too. Their car was blown up. I was not a young child, though. I had just finished sixth-form."

"That must have been dreadful. I'm very sorry for your loss."

"And I for yours."

"How did you…..?" Nell stopped. *Get over it* sounded wrong. Perhaps he had not got over it.

"We were in England at the time, with our grandparents, my brothers and sisters and I. The only way I could deal with this loss was by thinking of them, of how I could ease their pain. I couldn't, really, but I tried. This was not unselfishness. This was survival instinct. To ease other people's pain was to distract me from my own. It's why I became a doctor."

Nell said: "I was alone at home when the policeman came. He left me to tell my mother the news. I've lost other people since, of course, my mother, my aunt who helped to bring me up, my husband. But it's that first one that stays with me."

"Death isn't always sudden and untimely. It can be peaceful. But one cannot get over the fear of death without thinking about it, any more than one could get over a fear of spiders by never seeing any. That is why I have planned my funeral already."

"You have? "Nell was astonished.

"Yes, with the help of your brother-in-law, Reverend Bolton."

"But you're not old!" protested Nell. "Stanley's much older-I mean he's…well, he's not likely to be around when you…"

"No, but I'm sure he will leave a record of my wishes. Reverend Bolton knows his business well. I would recommend…" He stopped, seeing the anxiety reappear on the old woman's face. "Don't waste your energy on avoiding thinking about death. Think about it every day, then say: But I'm still here now. How can I enjoy myself today? How can I help someone else? Your family, for example, and your friends. If the worst thing about death for you is suddenness and shock how can you try to save *them* from the shock of yours?" He took her hand and gently pressed it. "Try not to worry, Mrs. Bolton. Things don't need to be as bad as you fear. And we are all here to help you."

As the doctor left, Nell lay down on her bed and closed her eyes. Well, she would do her best with the smoking. If the doctor was suggesting she should plan her funeral with Stanley, that wasn't going to happen. But her family, the people around her? Could she distract herself from her own fears by helping them?

She could hear Dr. O talking to someone outside her door, and wondered vaguely who it was. Then she must have dozed off for a few seconds, because she woke with a jolt. There was someone in her bedroom.

"Doctor's got your cigarettes,"said a familiar voice. "He said no smoking till after Friday at the earliest. We'll just have to make do with these."
Agnes stood at the end of the bed, holding up a packet of current buns.

33

My dear Raymond typed Nell. What next? Not "Thanks for your letter."When had Raymond last written to her? Had he ever written to her? Once, on a postcard, from cub camp, no doubt with Akela standing over him; once or twice during National Service to her and Clive, telling them his cricket scores. (After only a few weeks of square-bashing, Raymond had been sent to Cambridge to learn Russian and bat for the first eleven.) Since then, she only remembered the occasional brief note, giving her advice about money or notifying her of a change in his circumstances.

What did Nell want to say to her son? She had never known what to say to Raymond: how to stop him flying into rages, when, as a little boy, he had not got his own way; later, when his shirt collars were not clean, his trousers not pressed. The rage that Nell could not forget, but never wanted to think about, had been with his father. "Some father you are!" Raymond had yelled at Clive. "You've ruined my life!"

In fact, Raymond's life had not been ruined by his father's imprisonment for fraud and the collapse of the company he had founded and in which he had persuaded his son to join him. Raymond had moved away, found other sponsors, and succeeded brilliantly in his career, somehow quietly shaking off the stigma attached to his family. But those words, spoken when, devastated and betrayed, he believed that it had, were the last ever addressed by Clive's eldest child to his father.

Nell tried to convince herself that the estrangement between the two men did not include her, and in theory it did not. After Clive's death, Raymond had occasionally visited her in London. She had even visited him a few times in the large, comfortable, expensive London flat he shared with his wife, Eleanor. Yet Nell felt a reserve there, a resentment that had not existed before.

Nell wondered if Raymond and Eleanor were happy. Imogen claimed that they avoided contact with each other every morning before going out to work. "They're not morning people, either of them," she said. "They might kill each other. But by evening they've got over it. Ray cooks lovely dinners for them both." "He'd only ever eat sausage and mash, at home." objected Nell. "Yes, well he couldn't stand Eleanor's cooking, so he went on some posh course and learned to make pommes dauphinoise and….some sort of fancy sausages I suppose, with *jus* instead of lumpy Bisto gravy. Eleanor was only too happy to relinquish the wooden spoon, apparently."

Failure to cook for her husband had knocked Eleanor down a bit in Nell's estimation; that and the registry-office wedding with a bare minimum of guests (not including the groom's mother); but most of all, Raymond's dismissal of the idea that they might have children as something Eleanor did not want. Yet in spite of all that, Nell liked her daughter-in-law and found her much easier to talk to than her son.

She put a fresh sheet of paper into the typewriter.

My dear Eleanor,

I thought I would write, as it's a while since I saw you both. I hope all the work on the flat is finished now. It must have been very disruptive for a few weeks. I'm sure the Interior Designer you hired must have been helpful in getting everything right. (This was tongue in cheek. Nell thought it an absurd extravagance to pay someone else to design your own living space.)

I have settled very well into my new home. I miss my old friends, of course, but have made new ones, and am finding interesting things to do: not least,organising a concert and writing a sketch to be performed by the rest home residents! The thing is though, my health hasn't been all it could be lately. Nothing too bad, just a bit of chest trouble, and I'm on the mend now. I thought Raymond ought to know, though, so perhaps you would tell him?You can tell him I'm off the cigarettes now. I know he doesn't like me smoking.

Tell him not to worry, (he always was a worrier),and not to work too hard,and be sure to give him all my love.

I would love to see you both if you can manage a visit. I know how busy you are.

Much love,

Mum(-in-law)

P.S. Why not come to our concert at the end of this month. I'm going to invite Imogen. I don't suppose she'll be able to make it, though, with her family commitments.

34

My Dear Jonathan, began Nell, and paused. Her younger son preferred to be called Jon, but she hated to shorten names. *I hope you're still enjoying the sunshine. The surfing sounds great fun for you. It wouldn't be my cup of tea, as you know. Do be careful in the water, dear.*

Are you still seeing that young lady you mentioned, the one you met at the side of the road,whose car had broken down?It was most kind of you to stop and help her, but just what I would expect of you. Mandy, I think you said her name was. You also mentioned Jo, that you work with.

I know you'll think I'm an interfering old matchmaker, but it would be lovely to hear that you'd settled down with a nice girl.

Nell would much prefer her son to settle down with a girl in England, of course, but hadn't he said that Mandy was English? So there was hope. Mandy: the name sounded friendly.

I think you ought to know, dear, that I've not been well lately. Nothing too much to worry about though. I'm cutting down on cigarettes, which should help!

Are you still getting good tips at work, and is it still as busy? Some of the customers sound interesting characters, if a litte rough round the edges!

Please send some photos of Mandy, and Jo of course, if you have them, and the boys you go surfing with. I'd love to see what your friends look like.

All my love
Mum

P.S. Do NOT go after the job on the crocodile farm! It sounds far too dangerous!

To her daughter, Imogen, Nell did not write, because Imogen phoned dutifully every Friday afternoon at 3pm, before going out to meet the children from the school bus, sounding depressed and anxious, the latter because, Nell thought, Owen was probably standing over her, worrying about the telephone bill. He did not like the fact that his wife could not telephone her mother after 6pm, when calls were cheaper, because the calls came through to the office, which was closed in the evening.

Imogen knew that her mother was ill because the previous Friday Nell had sat in the office shivering and coughing, and struggling to concentrate on her daughter's complicated tale about Aled getting into trouble with a teacher over an inkwell (did people still use inkwells?) until Alison had taken over the phone and told Imogen that Nell needed to go back to bed. Imogen managed to phone again the following Monday, while Owen was away at sheep dog trials. Nell was feeling better and had been enjoying the conversation, but then her daughter had gone into lecturing mode about health care, and she had felt suddenly exhausted.

35

Agnes and Nell ran through the script together, before the rehearsal. It had been changed a little from the original version. Janet, who was not keen on developing a stage career, had been excused from taking part and instead given the task of organising the other parts of the concert.

THE COMMITTEE HAS DECIDED

<u>Scene 1</u>

Nell: Reverend Bolton, ladies and gentlemen as you all know, we are meeting here to discuss and plan our annual outing. As chairwoman of this committee-"

Alf: *Char*woman did she say? I need a charwoman. I need me mantelpiece dusting, and a good sweep under t'bed."

Nell:, As *chair*woman of this committee, I have drawn up an agenda, which you will see in front of you. The first item is: deciding where we want to go. Matron?

Matron: Well, one possibility is the seaside…..

(*Agnes plays a few bars of "Oh I do like to be beside the seaside" on the piano .)*

Matron: Yes, thank you Agnes. So who would like a seaside outing?

Gladys: Ooh, I would! We had lovely trips to Scarborough when I were a kid. Paddling in t'sea, eating winkles with a pin, donkey rides.

Eric:We used to go with t'Working Men's Club. Soon as we got there, me dad disappeared into t'pub. We'd no money for dinner-just a jam sandwich each, and I got a hiding for losing me boots in t'sea.

(*Alf plays imaginary violin while humming a mournful tune.)*

Eric: A lot of people go to Spain these days

Alf : Majorca !You wouldn't catch me though. Don't want a gippy tummy from eating snails.

Gladys: That's France.

Eric: It isn't . Majorca's not France.

Gladys: No, France is where they eat snails. They eat snails in France, not Majorca. And frogs' legs.

Alf: Disgusting.

Eric: Do you think they really do?

Gladys: Do what?

Eric: Eat frogs' legs?

Gladys: Not in Majorca.

Eric: No, in France. Do you think they really eat frogs' legs in France?

Joanna: I think we can forget about Majorca and France. It's a day trip we're planning.

Derek: (*Very slowly.)* We could, in theory, go to France and back in a day. When I went on my tour of Great Britain, using only my bus pass and the occasional train - very occasional you understand-in fact- (*Pauses, trying to remember.)*

Gladys: Shut up about your bus pass, Derek. You can't use your bus pass in France.

Alf: We're not going to France. I'm not eating frogs' legs and that sort of muck.

Derek: My point about the bus pass, was that I managed to reach Dover in fifteen hours, or were it sixteen? Somewhere between -travelling only by bus. I could, in theory of course, have reached Calais by ferry in a further, say, two hours, thereby-

Eric: Thereby not having time to get back again, in the same day.

Gladys: And no time to do anything when you got there.

Matron : Could we move on please!

Derek : My point is , though, we could get from *England* to France and back to *England* again in one day. Not back up here, you see, but back on English soil. Which in my book, Eric, constitutes GOING TO FRANCE FOR THE DAY!

Stanley: Gentlemen, please! Matron simply wants to find out how many of you would like to go to Scarborough for the day and how many would rather go to York, say, or somewhere in the countryside…

Eric : Miss Gillham would know, wouldn't she? You would know, wouldn't you Miss Gillham? I'm sure you've travelled a lot, and know a lot about t' world. (*aside in whisper to Alf*).Nell thinks she served in t' French Insistence.

Alf: Insistence on what?

Gladys: Resistance! He means the French Resistance

Derek: Oh well, French would have had to eat snails and frogs' legs and that during t'war. They would have been starving because of t'Nazi occupation.

Gladys: Oh, but they don't eat snails and frogs' legs from necessity. Those French people think they're a delicacy.

Stanley: We need an answer to the question…

Eric: Can you answer the question, Miss Gillham?

Priscilla: I -I'm afraid I don't know how many of us would prefer to go to York or to the seaside…

Eric: No no, that's not what we want to know.

Alf: He means, did you eat snails and frogs' legs and such when you was in t' French Insistence.?

Gladys: Resistance.

Priscilla: Ah…la Résistance…..mon cher Alphonse…..(*looks dreamy and mysterious as if remembering*)

Gladys: Ooh-er! Who's Alphonse?

(*Agnes strikes up la Marseillaise on the piano.)*

Alf: Bloody 'eck!

Eric : Alf! There's ladies present!

Alf: But bloody 'eck! Can't she play God save t' Queen? We'll be 'aving frogs legs for us dinner 'ere next!

Nell: Oh dear. Perhaps we'll get on better after a cup of tea.

(*Consults with Dr. O and Matron, then continues*)

…and since we don't seem to have made any progress at all with deciding where to go, after the break, Dr. O is going to tell us about his idea for a *healthy* outing for us all.

(*They all look at Dr O, who smiles and bows)*

Derek: Oh!

Eric: Oh, Dr O, eh?

Gladys: Eh?

(*They shuffle out, muttering about Os and As)*

"Was Priscilla really in the French Resistance?" asked Agnes, "and did she really have a lover called Alphonse?"

Nell laughed. "Oh, no, I made Alphonse up. And Priscilla was never in France, as far as I know."

It was extraordinary, to Agnes's rather literal way of thinking, that Nell could invent people and situations as if out of the air. "You're very clever Nell," she said, then blushed. Giving compliments was a thing she did so rarely it made her feel awkward. She continued hastily: "It's a bit disappointing though. Her not being in the Resistance, I mean."

"Well, I don't say she didn't do *any* war work, just not in France. I heard she did some radio propaganda broadcasting, something like that. She doesn't talk about it though."

"Or her lovers," said Agnes. "If she ever had any, that is. I mean, you invented Alphonse, but there could have been… She's not God's gift to men, nor am I, I know that. But-" Then a new thought struck her. "Perhaps Priscilla likes women," she said bluntly. "Perhaps she and Janet-you know, bat for the other side?"

This thought had occurred to Nell, but she was shocked to hear it mentioned openly. "I-I- didn't know they played cricket," she said, and this made them both laugh.

"Lets get on to scene two," said Nell.

Scene Two

Committee members all come back in and sit down.

Nell: Welcome back, ladies and gentlemen. I now ask Dr O to give us his recommendations for a healthy outing. Dr. O!

Dr.O: Thank you, Madam Chairman. I am very happy to share my suggestions for a healthy outing with you all. But I have to say that I'm less concerned about *where* you go on this outing, and am more interested in what you do when you get there.

Alf: Same as we do at'ome. Eat, drink. Sleep.

Bert: We won't just do that on t'outing, Alf. We need to get away from all that, that's whole point. Fresh air and exercise, that's what we need, i'n't it, Doc?

Eric: Fresh air makes me cough.

Alf: And we can't all do exercise. Some of us has a Hip.

Derek: I've got two hips.

Gladys: I've not got Hips. It's me feet that play up.

Derek: You must have hips, Gladys. Everyone's got hips.

Alf: Everyone has to have hips. Unless they haven't got legs, of course.

Derek: They would still need hips, Alf, even if they didn't have legs. We'd a neighbour next door, had no legs at all, but he still had hips.

Dr.O: Just sitting in the sunshine, on the sea front, will be good enough for those who have Hips. Those without Hips can take some gentle walks.

Bert: Not if they've not got hips, they can't. I can't imagine people without hips walking.

Alf: Oh no! People can't walk without hips. I should have thought you would know that, Doctor!

Gladys: (*to Derek*) How did your neighbour lose his legs, Derek? Was it the war?

Derek: Well now. There are different versions of that story…

Nell: Which we'd all love to hear later, Derek, but we really must move on..

Rev. Bolton: Yes indeed! We must not waste any more of Dr O's time, or Matron's. Let's have a straightforward vote, seaside or countryside! Madam Chairman?

Derek: Madam Chair*woman*, strictly speaking.

Alf: (*guffawing*) Or *char*woman!

Nell: Very well. All those in favour of a trip to the seaside, please raise your hands!

Derek: Objection!

Nell: What objection, Derek?

Derek: Gladys can't raise her right arm.

Gladys: I can't. I've got tennis elbow.

Eric: I had that once. Not that I ever played tennis.

Nell: What about the other arm, Gladys?

Gladys: I need that to hold me knitting wool.

Derek: It'll roll on t'floor else.

Nell: Well, Gladys, do you want to vote for seaside or countryside?

Gladys: Oh, I'm easy with either. As long as there's a souvenir shop. I always like to get a souvenir. I've got a hundred and five porcelain thimbles!

(*Sounds of admiration*)

Rev. Bolton: You'll be abstaining then, will you, Gladys?

Gladys: (*indignantly*) From buying thimbles?

Rev. Bolton: No! From voting!

Gladys: Oh no! I vote for seaside.

Alf: Me too. As long as there's a brass band.

Rev. Bolton: Good! That settles it. Scarborough it is!

Alf: *Scarborough!* Oh no! I've heard they've got that monkey disease in Scarborough.

Bert : They don't have monkeys in Scarborough, Alf. There's no zoo there.

Alf: I mean King Kong 'flu, that's what I mean. We wouldn't be able to go in souvenir shops, or fish and chip shops. Isn't that so, Dr. O? It wouldn't be safe, would it?

Dr. O: Well, it's true enough that there is a lot of Hong Kong 'flu about everywhere at the moment. But we can take precautions.

Derek: We should choose a country place then, where there's not so many people about.

Gladys: And no souvenir shops.

Eric: No fish and chips.

Alf: And no brass bands.

(Nell, Rev. Bolton and Matron all hold their heads in their hands and groan.)

Priscilla: Madam Chairman, Rev. Bolton, Matron, I have a proposal!

Alf: You've had a proposal? Was it from "Alphonse"?

Priscilla: Not that sort of proposal, Alf. What I mean is, I have a suggestion. Although, I must say, it was Alphonse who gave me the idea. It was when he visited my bedroom, earlier.

Gladys: Ooh!

Alf: Did he now!

Bert: Well I never!

Priscilla: He did. And then I saw him go past the window just now, and it reminded me.*(Everyone turns to* *look out of the window*) Oh, he's not there now. I expect he's gone to find his wife.

(*Everyone gasps in shock.*)

Gladys: His *wife*! Does she know he's been visiting your bedroom?"

Priscilla: Probably. I'm hoping he'll bring her to see me one day.

Rev. Bolton: Perhaps you would get to the point Miss Gillham. I'm sure we don't want to hear any more about Alphonse.

Gladys: Don't we? (*Rev. Bolton glares at her.)*

Priscilla: Well, Alphonse is a bit of a home bird, you see, unlike the Alphonse I named him after, who was with me in France in the Resistance. *He* went all over the place. Actually, I called all of them Alphonse. None of us used our real names anyway..

Gladys: How many were there?

Priscilla: Oh, I'm not sure I remember that, Gladys.

Rev. Bolton: If we could just get to the point, *please.*

Priscilla: As Alphonse was sitting there-

Gladys: Where was he sitting?

Alf: Was he… on the bed?

Priscilla: Of course not! He was by the window. As he was sitting there, I thought, *Alphonse is a home bird.*

Gladys: That's why he goes home to his wife.

Priscilla: Exactly. Well, I thought perhaps all of us are home birds too.

Eric: What's that got to do with the price of fish?

Priscilla: Well, since we've had such trouble deciding where to go, I thought perhaps we shouldn't go anywhere at all. It seems to me, most of us don't really want to go anywhere. But we can still have a treat. Here at Cherry Trees.

Eric: We could get fish and chips in.

Derek: So it does have something to do with the price of fish, you see.

Eric: What?

Gladys: Never mind. I could order a thimble from a catalogue!

Agnes: We could sing sea shanties!

Alf: We could get… a brass band!

Bert: Brilliant idea! The brass band can come here!

Gladys: Or Punch and Judy. I love a puppet show.

Bert: Punch and Judy's for kids.

Gladys: Oh, no, it isn't.

Eric: Oh yes it is. It's all hitting people with sticks and murdering babies.

Derek: And hanging people.

Bert: Kids' entertainment, like I said.

Gladys: Can't we have both? A brass band, if we must, *and* Punch and Judy?

Rev. Bolton: I'm afraid it would be much too expensive to have both.

Gladys: Let's have a vote then, Madam Chairman!

Nell: (*sighing)*Very well. All those in favour of a brass band, please raise your hands.

(*Eric, Bert, Alf, Rev. Bolton and Agnes raise their hands*.)

Rev. Bolton: I make that five, Nell.

Nell: Those in favour of Punch and Judy.

(*Gladys, Dr.O, Matron, Priscilla, and Derek raise their hands, but Gladys drops her knitting wool and Dr. O disappears under the table , looking for it.)*

Rev. Bolton: I make that four.

Nell: Four for Punch and Judy, five for a brass band. The decision of this meeting is that instead of an outing we stay here and have a day of treats, including a brass band-

Alf and Eric: Hurrah!

Nell: Rev. Bolton, Ladies and gentlemen I declare this meeting-

(*She is drowned out by Agnes striking up brass band music on the piano.)*

Alf: Let's have a practice, lads! Come on! (*They start to form a procession*.)

Nell: (*shouting*)I declare this meeting disBANDed!

(*Men march out to band music. Exit everyone else except Priscilla.)*

Priscilla: Good old Alphonse. I shall have to buy him some especially delicious birdseed, ready for his next visit to my bedroom windowsill..

CURTAIN

"Brilliant," said Agnes. "Love the ending .Wasn't expecting that.Why are you worried about it?"

"We need a song in there, for Dr.O, definitely. He's got a lovely singing voice. Have you heard it? That's why I wanted him in the sketch, for his singing voice. But I haven't found any suitable songs. I might have to make one up."

"I'm sure you'll manage, Nell."

"It's not just that though. Stanley won't be there today, at the rehearsal. I wish he was coming. I'm afraid he won't approve, and I'd rather find that out now. I don't want him to miss all the rehearsals and then turn up for the performance and start wanting to censor things."

Agnes wrinkled her nose up. "Well, if he doesn't come he's in no position to complain, is he? If he turns up on the day and starts raising objections, I'd tell him where to go. Somebody else could say his lines anyway, if they had to: Matron, for example. I'll say them if we're really desperate."

"I was thinking of leaving Matron out altogether. I'm not sure we need both her *and* Dr. O. And she said she'd rather recite a poem instead. Something about an Occasional Table."

"Sounds riveting," said Agnes. "The sketch is good Nell. Everyone else is happy with it, or if not, they haven't said so. If Stanley doesn't like it, he can do the other thing."

"His mother wouldn't have approved, that's for sure," said Nell, temporarily forgetting that her mother-in-law had been Agnes's great friend. It was true that the rest of the cast seemed happy with the script, especially the rest-home residents, even though it made mild fun of some of them. But Nell could not quite shake off the idea of Hannah, her mother-in-law, Stanley's sainted mother, looking down in disapproval on the two of them as they sat in her cottage , drinking sherry and planning a performance she would have thought scandalous.

"Hannah?"said Agnes, "I don't see why we should take any notice of what *she* might think. Don't get me wrong, I loved Hannah. She had many virtues, including being very good to me. But she was far too straight-laced. Victorian."

She paused for a moment and then said, diffidently, "I've had an idea. I could probably get hold of a French horn player. I've a few contacts in brass bands. Then we could put in some bits of brass band music, and drown you out properly at the end."

"Oh Agnes, that's a wonderful idea! Let's hope we can persuade him to come!"

36

When Agnes came home one evening from organ and choir practice at the Victoria Hall, Ted was looking out for her. "Strange woman," he said, "snooping round t'back. Spent a lot of time looking at your van." With Ted's recommendation, Agnes had bought the converted ambulance. It was now parked at the end of Ted's long backyard, on some hardstanding near the sliproad that ran around the backs of the houses. Ted had agreed to give it an overhaul. " I was just going out to send her packing,"he said, "and she went off. Forty-ish, medium height. Friend of yours, is she?"

" Light-brown hair, scraped back?"asked Agnes. "A bit scruffy?" But these were not things that Ted was in the habit of noticing. "It was getting dark."

"If it's who I think it is, she's most definitely no friend of mine," said Agnes, "and she's sure to be up to no good. If she comes again, tell her you'll call the police. Or – spray her with car paint, or something."

It was around twelve noon on the following day that Agnes found a note on the hall mat:

Dear Agnes,

I see you've bought a campervan! Looks a bit of a wreck to me- how did they get you to part with your money? You must have plenty to throw around, is all I can say. Old women living alone need to be careful they don't get taken advantage of. Oh but, of course, you know that from experience. And you weren't even old, then! The

good news is though, you have a step-daughter (well, almost step-daughter, if you insist on being pedantic) to look out for you. Here's an offer. Get the van insured, if it isn't already. Make sure it's covered for fire risk.Park it somewhere quiet-side of the road maybe. I'll see to the rest and we can share the proceeds. Think about it Agnes- we're family, after all, and we have to stick together, don't we?
Hope to hear from you soon
Rosamund.

37

"Your mother's not been well. She wants you to visit. Well, I think she wants me to visit, really. But I'm not sure I can get away from work.." Eleanor was scrupulously dutiful about making parental visits every six months, or at least, making sure that they happened, alternating between her own parents and Raymond's. It was definitely going to be Ray's mother's turn in a few weeks' time.

Her husband had his desk-tidy on the table in front of him and was sorting the pencils into groups of similar length and hardness. " Damn it," he said. "I've only one HB in the short ones, and one F. Do I put them with the other Fs and HBs, or keep them together in a separate compartment?"

"I should do that," said Eleanor, not having taken in what the exact question was.

"But it would occupy a whole compartment without filling it. All that wasted space!"

"Ray, did you hear what I've just told you? Your mother's been ill. We should go and see her.Or you should, anyway."

"She could come here."

"We'd have to fetch her in that case."

"She came on the underground last time."

"That was two years ago. It was a struggle for her then. She's bad on her feet now and she's been ill. And

Sheffield isn't on the London Underground, strangely enough."

"Sheffield?"

"It's where your mother lives now."

"Ah, yes." Raymond had temporarily forgotten that fact. "Well then, you're right, of course. I'd better go and see Mother."

38

"Jon, you can't leave me here. You just can't." Mandy gulped and gasped the words out. She had finished yelling at her "useless excuse for a boyfriend", and was now crying.

Oh, believe me, I really can, Jonathan wanted to say. These histrionics were only unusual in their intensity. A milder version happened nearly every day. Mandy acted more like a teenager than a thirty-eight-year-old woman. How did I end up with her, he wondered, on a God-forsaken crocodile farm in the middle nowhere? *You thought she was beautiful and sexy,* he answered himself. *And nice.* Maybe he'd been right about the first two qualities, but he'd discovered that Mandy was not nice, and that rather cancelled out her other attractions for him.

"Why can't your mother come out here?" she demanded. "My parents did."

"Your parents are loaded. They'd do anything for…" He bit back the words: "their little princess," but it was how he was beginning to see Mandy: entitled, bored, rich girl who wanted adventure, but couldn't take the hardships that went with it. She'd been as miserable as sin since they'd arrived at the crocodile farm. Nothing suited her: the heat, the humidity, the midges, the bunk rooms, the other workers. Not that he was finding it much fun himself.

"Anyway, Mum can't travel," he said. "She's never been out of the U.K. And she's ill. I need to see her."

"That letter took three weeks to reach you. She's probably better by now.She can't expect you to drop everything just because she's got a bit of 'flu. How selfish is that?"

"You don't know her. She never complains when she's ill. She wouldn't exaggerate it. It's much more likely she's a lot worse than she says, or she wouldn't mention it at all. I've got a bad feeling about it."

"You've also got no money." This was not entirely true. Jonathan had enough for his fare home, but not back again. He would lose his job if he took leave from it now. There was a good chance that if Jonathan went home now he would not get back to Australia.

"You could just phone her."

"Not that easy, is it?"

There were problems with the lines in this remote part of Australia.. Also, all calls had to be made from the office on the farm, and received in the office at Cherry Trees: obviously impossible because of the time difference. Besides, his mother might lie and tell him she was fine when she had been given only a week to live. He would phone his aunt and uncle, and hope that Doris would answer the phone; Stanley had always seemed to him the disapproving uncle, who might give him a lecture on wasting his life on dead-end jobs in company with unsuitable women. .

He looked at Mandy, stretched out on her bunk now, under mosquito nets, sulking. She showed no sign of getting up.They were both due back at work five minutes ago. He would have to cover for her again, somehow.

Maybe he wouldn't, though. Maybe he'd just let her get sacked.

He worked out that the phone call would have to be after 3pm but before 5pm (when the farm office closed) if he didn't want to disturb his aunt and uncle's sleep. This meant taking time off work, never popular with the foreman.Too bad, it had to be done. It was a matter of life and death, he'd tell them.

He was getting his boots on when Mandy suddenly sat up and said: "I'll come with you. I'll get Dad to pay for both of us." She laughed. "Don't phone. We'll surprise them! Let's just go, now! I can't wait to get out of this dump, anyhow.

39

Agnes played a few notes on the electric keyboard and frowned. “Nothing like a proper piano,” she grumbled. “But at least it’s not out of tune, which is more than you can say about that tinny thing in the drawing room.” She and Nell were in the chapel, supervising the cherry trees caretaker and handiman in last minute preparations for the show.

Alison from the office put her head around the door. “Visitors for you Nell!”

“My daughter?”asked Nell, hopefully. Imogen had said she would try to come for the concert, perhaps with Ffion.

Alison shook her head. “Three gentlemen. Young ones have unpronounceable names. Old one seemed too knocked out to speak. I had to get him a glass of water.” She sounded disapproving, as if this was somehow Nell’s fault. “They’re on the bench in your garden. I thought they’d better sit down while they wait. I’ll go back and tell them you’re coming.”

It was while Nell was ministering to Joseph, who, incredibly, had arrived with Abdullah and Jelilee, in a hired car driven by the latter, that Imogen and Ffion arrived. Nell’s delight in receiving these visitors was tempered by her anxiety about feeding them all and managing to complete the concert preparations. But Nell had never been averse to deputising. Ffion, suffering with excruciating teenage embarrassment in the presence of an exotic stranger, was sent with Abdullah to help Agnes in the chapel, while Jelilee and Imogen were dispatched to buy fish and chips. Joseph dozed gratefully in Nell's chair, with his feet up, while Nell brewed tea and searched for clean cups, feeling pretty exhausted herself, but happy.

Agnes, meanwhile, had lost her two Cherry Trees staff helpers, who had gone to their lunch, and was exasperated by the new additions to her team: a petite, delicate-featured teenager with skin so pale and hair so white-blond she looked like a fairy, and a dark-haired, bearded man about twice her size. The girl seemed terrified of her own shadow and unsure what to do when Agnes gave her the simplest of tasks, like putting a programme on every chair. Abdullah, on the other hand, on learning that Agnes wanted furniture moved, set about it with enthusiasm, putting most of it in the wrong place.

Agnes was relieved when the pale, blond girl's pale, blond mother, who explained that she was Nell's daughter, arrived and took her helpers away to eat fish and chips. "You're welcome to come too," said Imogen. There's plenty." But Agnes had no wish to involve herself in the melee at Nell's Cottage and explained in martyred tones that she would have to stay and finish the preparations on her own, since everyone else was busy.

40

The show-or concert, as Nell and Agnes liked to call it, was due to begin at 3pm. It was not intended to be long. In the first part, Joanna was going to recite her poem about the occasional table, which she had agreed to do in addition to taking part in the sketch. Dr. O was scheduled to sing two songs. Both were in a Ghanaian dialect, so nobody would understand them, but his voice was so beautiful that hopefully, nobody would mind. The child of a staff member was going to recite a poem by A.A. Milne. Next, there would be songs from members of the Victoria Hall choir, with some of which the audience would be able to join in. The first part would finish with a country-dance display by a small group of children from the local primary school. Janet was quite proud of the role she had played in securing this dancing troupe. After this, there would be a ten-minute comfort break, but no refreshments. Nell's sketch would make up the short second part of the concert. This meant that the table could be set up during the interval, and the cast, including Priscilla in her wheelchair, would have time to settle themselves round it.

After the performances, sandwiches and cake would be served. Janet was in charge of the tea urn, to be assisted by Doris, and was also on the door, taking money as the audience came in.

In the chapel, the communion table and the area around it had been screened off. A small portable platform and a microphone had been set up for the individual performers, but the platform was to be removed, to make space, before the dancing children and the choir did their bits. Matron was especially concerned that it should be well out of the way before her elderly residents performed their sketch: Heaven forbid that any of them should fall off it.

Stanley had been appointed master of ceremonies. When he arrived at 2.45pm, the chapel was filling up with people. Those of the Cherry Trees residents who were able to come filled up the front rows. Joseph, pleading deafness, had been allowed to sit there too. The rest of the audience was made up of staff, relatives and friends of the residents, the children's parents, and a few local people who had drifted in. Stanley noticed his wife, and Nell's daughter and granddaughter, on the back row, apparently in conversation with the two tall, dark young men next to them, one of whom was vaguely familiar. To his shame, he struggled to remember his niece's name, and the name of her daughter eluded him completely.

By 3pm, all the seats were taken. The country dance troupe sat on the floor at the front, the girls wearing brightly-coloured skirts, the boys embarrassed and fidgeting in waistcoats and cravats.

Stanley ignored the microphone, despising such new-fangled modern contraptions. He stood in front of it, shushed the fidgeting children and welcomed the audience. What they were about to see, he told them, was a concert organised by two remarkable and determined women, Miss Agnes Greystone, whom many of them would know from her role as organist and choir mistress at the Victoria Hall, and Mrs. Nell Bolton, a resident in one of the Cottages, and his sister-in-law. He added that Nell had written the sketch that would take place in the second half, in which several of the Cherry Trees residents would be taking part, and Agnes had arranged the music.

"I shall leave you to make up your own minds, of course," he concluded, "but I am sure that when you have seen this concert, you will agree that it has been a great achievement on the part of these two ladies , and everyone involved."

Joanna, terrified that she was going to forget her lines, recited her poem about the occasional table without mishap, and received enough laughs and polite applause to feel pleased with herself.

Dr. O sang unintelligibly but beautifully, and the girl who recited "The King's Breakfast," did so well, she was asked for an encore. That went less well: she recited the first verse twice, then realising her mistake, gave up altogether. She was roundly applauded nevertheless. The country-dancers lined up in the space provided for them, looking very solemn. They were forced to stand there for some minutes while a dispute took place, in muted tones, between Agnes and the children's teacher, about the music. This was eventually resolved by Agnes relinquishing all responsibility and allowing the teacher to take her seat at the keyboard. But the teacher had noticed the serious faces of her troupe, and before sitting down, she went over and hissed at them to smile and look cheerful as they danced. This caused one child to pull his face into a distorted grin, and the rest to collapse into giggles. None of this prevented the children from dancing well, but they were a little too vigorous for some audience members. The floor shook, and the elderly occupants of the front row worried that they would be bumped into. There was relief all round when the dance was over and the children were dispersed to sit with their parents, or be taken home.

After the break, Stanley announced "The Committee has Decided". Nell crossed her fingers and prayed that no-one would forget to speak up, or lose their place in the script. Agnes struck up an introductory tune on the keyboard.

Nell need not have worried. Within a few minutes, the audience were laughing so much, they were obviously not going to care about a few mistakes.

Imogen was worrying about her mother. To her mind, Nell looked feverish, and seemed to sway on her feet at times. She looked at her aunt for an opinion, but Doris seemed not to have noticed. She and Ffion, either side of Imogen, were relaxed and enjoying themselves, as were the two Afghans, though it must have been difficult for them to understand all the jokes.

The French horn player, who turned out to be an inspired addition to the team, did his best to impersonate an entire brass brand on his own, and led the play to its triumphant almost-conclusion amid rapturous applause. Stanley had to intervene and ask for silence so that Priscilla, waiting patiently in her wheelchair, could make her final speech. This was followed by more laughter, more applause, and then the cast stood together and took their final bow. Nell, standing with them,was delighted with the success of the concert, but was beginning to feel woozy. Her head was muzzy and she longed to sit down on her own somewhere and smoke a few cigarettes. Stanley made an appreciative speech and the A.A.Milne-reciting child presented Nell and Agnes with bouquets of flowers.

Then Doris and Imogen were there, leading Nell to a seat and unnecessarily fussing, in her view. Ffion and the young men were despatched to fetch tea and refreshments. Joseph, who had slept through most of the sketch, and only woken when the French horn player had struck up, shuffled along to congratulate his old friend, and to ask for a script. This would help him to compose a poem in praise of the event, a copy of which he would send to Nell.

Nell drank two cups of tea straight off, but had no appetite for the food. Happy as she was to be surrounded by appreciative friends and family, she needed to be back in her Cottage, resting. But the walk back felt too daunting. Doris, guessing this, came to the rescue. “I’ll fetch the car up, Nell," she offered. "Stan and me are about to leave, anyway. We can drop you off."

Nell took leave of her London visitors, expressing much appreciation for the trouble they had taken in coming. Imogen and Ffion promised to visit the next day, before going home. She looked around for Agnes, but Agnes had disappeared.

41

Agnes was happy with the success of the concert, and rejoiced in the many compliments she and Nell received, but she had suddenly found the effort of socialising too much.

Besides, she wanted to get back to her van. Since Rosamund's note, she had not felt comfortable leaving it unattended. This was not rational, Agnes knew. She had not offered Rosamund any insurance money, so there would be no reason at all for Rosamund to damage the van. But that woman was capable of anything. Agnes went to check on the van where it was parked, in the corner of the small carpark in front of the Cottages. She had been in two minds about bringing it. It was roadworthy, and insured, but she had not driven it much yet. Still, this was a short, local journey, a good chance to practise, and if she and Nell were going to spend some time together after the concert, she might not want to cycle home in the dark.

Having reassured herself about her new vehicle, she pottered around Nell's garden for a bit. The weather had been dry and the plants needed water.

Then she sat in the van and waited for Nell's return. Watching from behind the curtain, as Nell was dropped off, Agnes locked the van carefully and went to knock on her door. "Come in!" called Nell, who had left the door on the latch, half-expecting her friend. "Sherry?" she suggested. "You'll have to pour it. I'm off my feet."

Agnes forgot about her intention to drive home later, telling herself vaguely that she would sort something out, and poured two double sherries. Now that the concert was over, she and Nell both excused themselves from the cigarette ban.

They drank a toast to everyone they could think of who had helped the show succeed, and basked in the satisfaction of success. Then Nell was fast asleep, her cigarette burning away in the ash-tray.

She woke briefly when Agnes got up to put the kettle on, and coughed
so violently, that Agnes hurried to fetch some water and Fisherman's Friends.

"You should go to bed, Nell."

"Yes, yes, I must."

"Shall I help you?"

Nell shook her head

"I'll make some tea, then. You can drink it in bed if you want. Then I'll leave you in peace." Agnes washed a few dishes while the tea brewed, then put a cup beside Nell, who was still in the chair. She threw a rug over Nell's legs. If she wasn't going to go to bed, she had at least better keep warm. Then Agnes tidied round a bit and emptied the ash-trays, said "Goodnight" and left.

For some reason she did not take the door off the latch; and for that, she would be eternally thankful.

The camper van was not really ready for sleeping in, but she did have a couple of rugs and some cushions that had come with it: a bit smelly, but beggars could not be choosers. Agnes wrapped herself in the rugs and lay down on the bench. If she could sleep off the sherry for an hour or so she might be fit to drive home.

She dozed a little but was suddenly wide awake again. Thoughts began buzzing in her head: the concert, the van, Nell's cough, which was worrying: and behind it all, in the darkness of the empty carpark, she could not shake off the idea of Rosamund lurking around, with evil intent.

Then she smelled smoke.

42

"Why am I here?" Nell had woken to find an oxygen mask over her face, which the nurse had temporarily removed.

"You were brought in last night, Mrs. Bolton, don't you remember? Smoke inhalation. It's affected your lungs. Only a bit, though," she tried to reassure the patient. "It was more of a precaution, they said."

"Oh yes." There had been smoke in her flat. She had been struggling to breathe-that was frightening- and Agnes had gone over to Cherry Trees to call an ambulance, and come back with Joanna and they had made her get out of bed and sit in the bathroom with the hot water running. They'd said something about a fire in the pedal bin, which Agnes had put out. "Oh dear, I shall need a new peddle bin, shan't I?" She smiled at the nurse, who perhaps thought that that might be the least of her worries.

Later, when she was dozing, Nell woke to find a pretty, slim blond girl standing by the bed. Nell pulled her mask down. "Ffion," she whispered. "Goodness, you've grown."

"It's Fiona," said the girl, adding unnecessarily: "My mum's English," as if Nell might not have known that.

Good for you, thought Nell. *You don't have to go along with all that Welsh nonsense.*

"It's lovely to see you dear, " whispered Nell, and held out a hand to her granddaughter, who took it and sat down on the only chair, so that their interlinked hands rested on the bedclothes.

"Is your mother…? And the others..?" Nell looked around the room.

"It's just me and Mum. She's gone to get stuff from the shop. Nest and Aled are staying with Mum's friend. We came for the concert, remember?"

The concert. It seemed like a century ago.

"That sketch was brilliant, Gran. I couldn't stop laughing. I didn't know you were so clever, Gran."

They beamed at each other.

"Did your mother enjoy it?"

"You bet she did. "

"I'm glad. You came a long way."

"Mum was going to come and see you anyway, because Auntie Doris told her you hadn't been well. Then she remembered the concert. And also she wants to show you her book. Did you know she's written a book? Well, it's your book really."

"Mine?"

"You know those stories you used to make up for us when we were little? The one about a runaway horse, and a fairy whose wand got stolen by the wicked witch…"

"You-remember- them- better-than me dear," wheezed Nell.

"Well, Mum's written them all down now, and her friend's drawing pictures for them. They want to get them published. Anyway, she's going to show you them. And then she decided she was going to get here in time for the show, because she remembered the funny sketches you wrote for the Brownies when she was a kid. And I said I wanted to come. Auntie Doris liked it too, and Uncle Stan liked being in it, though he pretended not to. We stayed with them last night, and we were going to go home today, but then… they said you're not well."

Stan thinks your mother hasn't got much longer was what Doris had said bluntly to Imogen. *He says her breathing's very laboured.* Fiona, overhearing this, had not understood what "laboured breathing" meant, but now she did. Her grandmother's breathing was definitely laboured, and it began to disturb the child.

"I'll just go and find Mum," she said, but then realised her grandmother had fallen asleep again, and she crept silently out of the room.

Nell dreamt of Fiona and Nest and Aled when they were very small, listening to Nell's stories in the chilly attic bedroom where their father seemed to think it was all right for them to sleep. Nell thought they should at least have hot-water-bottles, if they had to sleep in this unheated section of the old farmhouse. She began to feel shivery herself, but hot at the same time, and woke with a jolt.

"Hello Mum," said Imogen, sniffing hard and kissing her mother on the cheek. "I didn't mean to wake you, sorry. Ffion's gone for a little walk. She needed some fresh air."

"Have you-got-a cold, dear? Your- eyes- look…"

"Hayfever. Lots of flowers out there."

"Your book," said Nell. "Fiona said-you want -to show me."

"There's nothing to show yet really, but I can describe it. It's mostly the stories you used to tell the children. Only in Welsh. It's for children learning Welsh in school. My friend's done some illustrations."

Nell wanted to help somehow, to encourage her daughter, to give her advice about where to submit her work, but she knew nothing about Welsh books, so she just said:"Very pleased-you're doing-something else, dear. Not housework, not farm, something else. And so pleased to see you." Within a few seconds, she was asleep again.

43

Nell was dreaming. She was at school, and it must have been the end of term because the girls were not sitting at their usual forms but on chairs in a circle, where they sat to play games, like "The Minister's Cat". The teacher had Dr. O with her, and he suggested the next game should be about thinking up euphemisms for dying and he started it off by saying: "I am going to join the choir eternal". The teacher said: "But you can't sing," and it made the girls laugh. Then Grace Chadwick tried to quote Shakespeare, but couldn't get it right. "I'm going to shuttle-shuttle off this mortal-something-" "Shuffle," Nell corrected her. "Shuffle off this mortal coil."

"What was that, Nell?" Stanley was sitting by her bed, leaning over to catch her words.

"Shuffle- off this- mortal coil," repeated Nell. "Not me, Grace Chadwick. Do you think she will?" she added anxiously.

"We'll have to wait and see," said Stanley noncommittally. He was accustomed to the wandering minds of the delirious. "Doris is here. I'll leave her to sit with you a bit."

Doris took Nell's hot hand in hers, and Nell drifted back into sleep.

When she woke, Doris had gone and Stanley was there again. "I'm wondering, Nell," he said, "if you would like me to pray with you."

Too tired to think how to say "no" politely, Nell considered pretending to fall asleep again. But there were things she wanted to say to Stanley. "Thank you, Stanley," she said. "For the sketch, I mean." *For not disapproving, for taking it all in good part, for being a sport and joining in the spirit of the thing* was what she meant, but that was too many words.

"No need to thank me for that, Nell. It was fun."

Too weak to sit up Nell showed her surprise only by turning her eyes to look at him. She had never before heard her brother-in-law talk about fun. He did have a sense of humour, that was true, but it was more of the ironic type.

"We all had fun," he continued. "Matron told me everything you've done for the residents, Nell. She said you cheered them up, took them out of themselves, got them to do things they never thought they could. I'd say that concert last night was an amazing achievement. It's we who should be thanking you."

Nell saw that he was sincere and was warmed by the praise. "Well," she said, modestly, "there was Agnes…"

"Who would never have done it without you," interrupted Stanley. "It's amazing what you've done for Agnes, too. You've transformed that woman!" He thought then that he had underestimated his sister-in-law, and that perhaps he should apologise for that, but he was not sure how to. But Nell was smiling, clearly pleased by what he'd said, so perhaps there was no need.

"Agnes - is a funny old thing," said Nell. "But she's been a good - friend to me." She hesitated, realising, with slight panic, that she had said "has been," not "is". *But she had better not duck out of what else she needed to say. Dr. O would want her to carry on.* Stanley, aware that she had something important to say, was waiting patiently.

"When I am - gone," she began, heart pounding, not liking to hear her own words.

"Yes, Nell," said Stanley encouragingly, "when you are with the Lord, and at peace…" He almost added, "which perhaps will not be long now," but thought better of it.

"I want-I would like -Agnes to have the Cottage. It's yours, I know. Not my decision. Piano, though." She was running out of breath. "Agnes-not old-but piano."

Stanley smiled. "You'll be pleased to know, Nell," he said, "I'd come to that decision myself."

44

Raymond left his car in the hospital visitors' carpark and walked towards the front entrance. His palms were already clammy, and he wasn't even inside yet. At any moment an ambulance might come screeching up to the door, and they'd be carrying some unfortunate victim in, just as Raymond himself was about to enter. A taxi drew up in the space next to the one reserved for ambulances and two people got out: a woman with pink hair that looked as if it hadn't been brushed for years, and psychedelic trousers. The man with her was long-haired and bearded. *Aging hippies* thought Raymond scornfully.

"Ray!" The hairy man was approaching him, arms outstretched. Was he about to be kidnapped and taken to a Moonie colony?

"Jonathan!"

"It's been a long time. I'm a bit hairier now." Jonathan embraced his brother. "It's good to see you. This is Mandy."

"Hi, Jon's brother," said Mandy.

Raymond nodded stiffly.

"How's Mum, do you know?" asked Jonathan as they walked towards the hospital doors.

"Getting worse, according to Uncle Stan. He thinks she hasn't got much time. But that's only what he thinks." Raymond had never had much time for his uncle.

"Have you been before to see her? Do you know what ward she's in?"
Raymond shook his head. "I've just driven up here from London."

When they eventually found the ward, only one of them was allowed in to see Nell. "Two visitors per patient, and there's someone with her already. You can use the visitors' room at the end. There's a drinks machine."

"You go," Raymond told his brother. I'll get a cup of coffee." The unbrushed girlfriend followed him into the visitors' room, so he felt he had to offer her a coffee. She shook her head. Then she had to help him work the coffee machine. Would he have to sit next to her? Please God, no! She was offering him a cigarette. She was obviously going to light one up herself. The room was already quite smoky from other visitors. Raymond was wondering if he could escape through the glass door marked "fire exit" on the excuse of needing fresh air, when a large woman with short grey hair put her head around the visitors' room door.

"Raymond Bolton?" she enquired, sounding like she had a bad cold. Raymond raised a hand. "Your brother said to tell you, I've come out now, so you can go in to your mother. Nurse'll tell you where she is." Raymond frowned. Surely a woman with a bad cold shouldn't be visiting his mother? But he said nothing, took a swig of the awful coffee and left. "I'll have that if it's still going." Agnes had spotted the proffered cigarette, and lost any inhibition she might have had about begging from a stranger. She needed a smoke. Also, she had no idea who this hippy woman was, but it had crossed her mind that hippies were likely to know about camper vans.

45

Nell lay on her bed, propped up by pillows; tubes, it seemed, going into every conceivable part of her body, which Raymond did his best not to notice. Jonathan sat by the bed, holding her hand. Her eyes were closed, but she opened them when her elder son came in. He kissed his mother on the cheek.

"Raymond, how lovely," whispered Nell. Raymond was shocked at the weakness of her voice. Jonathan fetched him a chair, and they sat either side of the bed, each holding one of their mother's hands. They were both afflicted by hay fever, Nell thought. There must be an epidemic. She tried to think of conversation topics, but the effort of speech seemed too much, and she closed her eyes again. Nevermind. It was good enough that they were both here, her two sons here together, not arguing, holding her hands in theirs. *They will remember this,* she thought, *they will remember me.* "Remember me when I am gone…" The words of a Christina Rosetti poem she had had to learn at school came drifting into her mind. She had not liked that poem, which was about remembering *and* forgetting, and was definitely morbid. She must banish it from her thoughts. She must think positively. "It may take some time. Things sometimes need to get worse before they improve," the hospital doctor had said when she had told him of her worry that she seemed not to be getting better. She was aware of Jonathan talking to her now, with Raymond occasionally joining in. She should make an effort to listen, but it was all so tiring.

Nell was vaguely aware of her sons leaving, promising to be back later, then she was asleep again. She was in the dark, narrow hallway of her childhood home, and she was finding it difficult to breathe. It was so, so stuffy. She began desperately gasping for air, but she dared not open the front door. Someone was knocking - the policeman! She would not open the door, at all costs.

The door flew open of its own accord. A dark figure stood there, a man in working clothes, covered in soot, holding a lantern. It was not the policeman. The street outside the door had become a dark railway tunnel, at the end of which a bright light shone. The man looked from Nell to the light, and back again, smiling. He raised the lantern, and held out his other hand to her.

“Don’t be frit, our Nell,” said Pa. “You’ll be grand.”

46

Stanley dictated to his secretary:

Dear Miss Greystone,

As you are, of course, aware, after the sad demise of my sister-in-law, Mrs. Ellen Bolton, the apartment which she occupied at the Methodist Homes has become vacant. As you are also aware, this apartment belongs to me personally, having been left to me by my mother.

Before she died, Nell expressed to me her wish that you should have the apartment, and this was also the wish of my late mother. I should like to add that, in appreciation of the enormous help you have given to both of these ladies, this is also my own heartfelt wish.

It is, of course, unusual for a person of your age who is not disabled to be offered a Cottage, but in this case there are exceptional circumstances. Your piano needs to be housed, and this is important, because your musical talents are a great asset to Methodist Homes and to the Church. Although I had no obligation to do so, the Cottage being my personal property, I have discussed this issue with the Board, and they are all wholeheartedly in agreement.

I have great pleasure, therefore, in offering you the tenancy of 1, The Cottages, Methodist Homes, Sheffield with immediate effect.

There is a sliding scale of rental charges for the apartments, details of which are on the enclosed sheet. However, the rent charged for Cottage 1 is entirely under my control, and I can assure you that we can come to an arrangement that is well within your means.

I look forward to your response to this offer.

Yours very sincerely,

Stanley Bolton (Rev.)
Superintendent,Methodist Church, Sheffield.

47

Stanley was not surprised that Agnes had come to see him, though he did think she might have contacted him by phone to reply to his letter. Well, perhaps it was as well that she was here in person, because he had some something to tell her that she might possibly find upsetting.

"Agnes," he began, as soon as they were seated, deciding that they knew each other well enough by now to dispense with formality. "I've had a bit of news. It's not what you came about, I know, but I think I ought to tell you. It's about Hubert Scully."

"Hubert?" Agnes had pressing things on her mind at that moment, and Hubert Scully was not one of them. "What's he done?"

"Had another stroke, though a minor one, I believe. I was contacted by our hospital visiting team. He – Hubert I mean – was anxious that I should be informed - and you, apparently."

"I don't know what anybody expects *me* to do."

"There isn't any reason why you should do anything at all, of course. But he wanted you to know, so I've told you."

"Is he in hospital?"

"I believe he's home now."

"With Rosamund.?"

"Well no, that's the thing. Rosamund has gone."

"Gone?"

"Yes, moved her things out. Hasn't been seen for days. Since Hubert went to hospital, in fact. I'm afraid it appears that she assaulted him. The neighbour found him on the floor, having banged his head, apparently. He said that she knocked him down, and I suppose there's no reason not to believe him."

A faint wave of sympathy, coming from somewhere in the past, began to stir in Agnes. "Perhaps I should…"

"Go and see him? Definitely not! Whatever you do, stay out of that man's clutches."

"If that's what you think.."

"I do. Now, to get on to pleasanter topics: I assume you came about the Cottage."

" No, I didn't." Agnes spoke quickly. "I've come to say something and you need to let me say it now, otherwise I shan't have the courage." Surprised, but sensing the importance of what his parishioner had to say, Stanley waited.

"Nell died of smoke inhalation, didn't she?"

"The death certificate said pneumonia."

"Yes, but brought on by inhaling smoke. It was my fault. I killed Nell. This offer of the Cottage-how could I possibly take it when I'm responsible for Nell's death?" Agnes began to sob.

"The smoke came from the fire in the pedal bin…"

"Exactly! I emptied the ash-trays! I put the cigarette ends in the bin. I don't know if it was Nell's or mine that wasn't properly out, and smouldered, but…"

"I heard you put the fire out with water from the garden hose, because the bin was on fire under the sink, and you couldn't reach it. That was quick thinking."

" I'd been using the hose earlier. I'd left it on the tap. That's not the point. I put the fire out, but I caused it. I didn't check those stubs before I put them in the bin. I should have made a point of checking them."

"Why didn't you make a point of it, Agnes?"

"I don't know."

"Yes, you do. Think about it."

"I suppose because it's usually something I do automatically. When I empty ash-trays, I always check everything's properly extinguished. I just always do."

"In other words, you don't need to make a point of it, because you do it automatically. Is there any reason to suppose that you didn't do it automatically on this occasion too? If you did, you wouldn't remember it would you? Things we do every day don't always register. Was Nell in bed when you left ?"

" What's that got to do with it? No. She was still in the chair. I put a rug over her."

"In that case it is perfectly possible, is it not, that Nell smoked another cigarette before she went to bed? It may not have been the ones you smoked together that caused the fire at all. She may have had another, and put it in the bin herself, for all anybody knows. I should stop agonising about cigarette ends, if I were you. It’s natural to feel guilty when someone dies, and ask ourselves how we could have prevented it. But mostly, we couldn’t. Nell died of pneumonia, and she was ill before that fire happened. Anyone could see that. Doris and Imogen were worried about her at the concert.”

Agnes said slowly: “Do you really not think it’s my fault?.”

“I really don’t.”

“I’m grateful for that, Reverend. And I’m grateful for the offer of the Cottage too, don’t think I’m not. But I don’t want it. Not because of the guilt, you’ve made me think twice about that. But I just don’t want it. Thank you. I can tell you who does, though.”

48

A few days later, Agnes received the following hand-written note from Stanley:

Dear Agnes,

I've been to see Hubert. He appears to have recovered reasonably well from the attack, and the stroke was a minor one and not too damaging. To be honest, though, I was not very familiar with his state of health beforehand, so I find it difficult to judge how much worse his condition might, or might not, be. He is living in the flat which he shared with his so-called daughter. I do not know how long he will be able to stay there, as it is a council flat, and is, it would seem, in her name. There is no sign of her, and Hubert does not believe she will come back. He claims that she found a stash of money that he had secreted away somewhere, and knocked him down when he tried to stop her making off with it. There is no way of knowing if any of this is true, of course.

Hubert wanted to see you, but I told him that he is not your responsibility in any way, and that if he wishes to communicate with you, he should do so through me. I shall only pass on any messages if you wish me to do so. Stop worrying about him, Agnes. He doesn't deserve it.

With very best wishes,

Stanley Bolton.

P.S:In case you were wondering, Hubert is managing to look after himself with the help of a neighbour who comes in every day. I fear she has submitted to his charms.

“Poor woman,” said Agnes. “Poor, stupid woman.”

49

On the Air Canada flight from Manchester to Toronto Agnes Greystone tore up her "Tell us How We Could do Better"card. She ripped through the words:"We hope you have enjoyed your flight with us, but we know we're not perfect, so please tell us about any improvements you would like us to make," which were followed by a list of tick-boxes.

Boring, thought Agnes, dropping the pieces into her empty coffee cup.. *Can't be bothered with that*. Did some people actually have nothing better to do than find things to complain about?

Agnes had enjoyed every second of her flight, intrigued by everything from the miniature meals in covered foil trays, each item in its separate compartment: an omelette in one, two small frankfurters in another, baked beans in a third, and the next containing a muffin with a portion of butter and jam, to the views from the windows, in which she was sometimes above the clouds, sometimes below them, once looking through darkness to the glimmering lights of a small coastal settlement on an island somewhere. What were all those people doing down there, while she was up here, looking at them? How could it be that in ten minutes of flying she could pass over thousands, perhaps millions, of people, all with their own thoughts and activities, possibly looking up at her plane and wondering who was in it.

Of course the seats were too small, and sometimes her fellow-passengers were inconsiderate, the flight stewards over-zealous, the temperature too hot/cold and it was far too noisy to sleep a wink, but who gave a toss about any of that when just being up there, flying above the earth, was so exciting?

In her current mood, if the pilot had suddenly announced that the plane was about to drop into the icy waters of the Arctic Ocean and be lost forever, Agnes might have still have thought her trip had been worthwhile.

She felt ready to tackle anything. If she didn't get on with her Canadian cousin and the cousin's family; if, having invited her to stay, they found they could not put up with her (Agnes was the first to admit this was a strong possibility), she would just take her leave and do something else.

When she got home again, she had her camper-van to look forward to. Ted had agreed to do it up for her, at a price. He'd also offered her a permanent parking space among the other vehicles that occupied the front and back yards around his house. Nell's son, Jonathan, after he split up with Mandy (who returned to her parents to be coddled), but before he went south to look for work, had gone out with Agnes in the van to help her get used to driving it, and had given her a lot of practical advice about gas bottles and water-pumps and other useful things.

The seatbelt lights came on, and the plane began to bank. “Ladies and gentlemen,” announced the pilot, “we are preparing to land.”

50

"You're going to sell it then, your mother's Cottage?" Doris looked at her husband in surprise. "I thought you said Nell wanted Agnes to have it, and you agreed with her?"

"I offered it to Agnes. She doesn't want it." He could not tell Doris about his interview with Agnes: as a minister, he had to observe confidentiality. So he said: "She doesn't seem so bothered about finding a more comfortable home now that she's got her camper-van."

"What about her piano?"

Stanley smiled. "The piano is taken care of. Agnes will be able to go and play it whenever she likes. By appointment of course, she can't just walk in. But the purchaser has agreed to look after it for her and let her have access. It was her idea, not mine. She suggested it."

"She must be a friend of Agnes, then?"

"I think you would say that. She plays the piano herself."

"Priscilla?"

"Miss Gillham, yes. She wants it for herself and her companion. Janet, isn't it? Janet lives in a house owned by Miss Gillham at the moment, but she thinks that, with the garden and so on, it's getting to much for Janet to manage. And, it seems, they want to be together."

"Yes," said Doris. "There was a bit of gossip about them recently. Something to do with cricket."

Stanley gave her a reproving look. "You know what I think about gossip, my dear."

"Sorry, Stan. It will be lovely for the two of them, as long as they can manage."

"They've worked all that out.The plan is to pay for a care assistant to come in every day. Miss Gillham isn't short of a penny, you know."

51

It was spring, and warm enough for Priscilla and Janet to have the French windows open. Out of them drifted the smell of freshly-baked scones, which Agnes inhaled as she walked from the carpark and entered the Cottage via the back garden. She always preferred to come in this way, and was delighted to see the flowerbeds covered in forget-me-nots. She would have to thin them out, though. There were far too many. Or would that be Janet's job now?

"Lovely to see you, Agnes! How was Canada?"said Priscilla.

"And how is the camper-van?"asked Janet.

"I'll show you later," said Agnes proudly. (Ted had spray-painted the van beautifully, and she had made new curtains and cushions.) "And I'll tell you all about Canada. But first things first!"

Agnes's piano had been moved from the former spare bedroom, which was now Janet's private domain. Space had somehow been found for it in the living room. Agnes took a seat and lifted the lid, played a few scales. Then: "This is for Nell," she announced, and the notes of Verdi's Grand Triumphal March from Aïda filled the room and rang out across the sunlit lawn.

Printed in Great Britain
by Amazon

46952082R00118